Yuri Aurealis

The son of a duke whose family, the Water Clan, is highly skilled at water magic. Yuri is an unrivaled child prodigy who has contracted with two first-class spirits. Normally cold and unsociable, he loosens up slightly around those he trusts.

Brigitte Meidell

The oldest daughter in the distinguished Fire Clan—and unfortunately contracted with a weak no-name spirit. Although her fellow students hate her after the foolish and haughty behavior she displayed to please her former fiancé, Joseph, in truth she's an excellent student with a keen mind.

If the Villainess and Villain Met and Fell in Love 1

-She Was All but Disowned for Her Spirit Contract, but She's Still Competing with Her Rival-

Harunadon　　*Illustration by* **Yomi Sarachi**

Brownie

A third-class spirit, contracted with Kira.

Joseph Field

Third Prince, Brigitte's former fiancé.

Lisa Selmin

A close friend of Joseph's.

Brigitte Meidell

Plays the role of a domineering, arrogant villainess.

Kira Anik

Brigitte's classmate.

Undine

A first-class water spirit, contracted with Yuri.

Ariel

A second-class wind spirit, contracted with Nival.

Yuri Aurealis

Shunned by other students because of his reputation as a genius, he plays the villain.

Nival Weir

President of Brigitte's class.

"It's nothing special. Just take it."

Uh, that's not true!

Clifford Yuize

The only servant Yuri opens up to.

"This seems like a gift you should give to a girl who means something to you…"

CONTENTS

Harunadon

Illustration by **Yomi Sarachi**

If the **Villainess** and **Villain** Met and **Fell in Love** 1

-She Was All but Disowned for Her Spirit Contract, but She's Still Competing with Her Rival-

YEN ON
NEW YORK

If the Villainess and Villain Met and Fell in Love

Met and Fell in Love

1

~She Was All but Disowned for Her Spirit Contract, but She's Still Competing with Her Rival~

Harunadon

TRANSLATION BY JUDY JORDAN ♦ COVER ART BY YOMI SARACHI

AKUYAKU REIJO TO AKUYAKU REISOKU GA, DEATTE KOI NI OCHITANARA vol.1
~NANASHI NO SEIREI TO KEIYAKU SHITE OIDASARETA REIJO WA, KYO MO REISOKU TO
KISOIATTE IRUYO DESU~
Copyright © 2021 Harunadon
Illustrations copyright © 2021 Yomi Sarachi
All rights reserved.
Original Japanese edition published in 2021 by SB Creative Corp.

This English edition is published by arrangement with SB Creative Corp., Tokyo in care of Tuttle-Mori Agency, Inc., Tokyo.

English translation © 2023 by Yen Press, LLC

Yen On
150 West 30th Street, 19th Floor
New York, NY 10001

Visit us at yenpress.com
facebook.com/yenpress ♦ twitter.com/yenpress
yenpress.tumblr.com ♦ instagram.com/yenpress

First Yen On Edition: October 2023
Edited by Yen On Editorial: Anna Powers
Designed by Yen Press Design: Liz Parlett

Yen On is an imprint of Yen Press, LLC.
The Yen On name and logo are trademarks of Yen Press, LLC.

The publisher is not responsible for websites (or their content) that are not owned by the publisher.

Library of Congress Cataloging-in-Publication Data
Names: Harunadon, author. | Sarachi, Yomi, illustrator. | Jordan, Judy, translator.
Title: If the villainess and villain met and fell in love / Harunadon ; illustration by Yomi Sarachi ;
translation by Judy Jordan.
Other titles: Akuyaku reijo to akuyaku reisoku ga, deatte koi ni ochitanara. English
Description: New York, NY : Yen On, 2023–
Identifiers: LCCN 2023028673 | ISBN 9781975375935 (v. 1 ; trade paperback)
Subjects: CYAC: Fantasy. | Villains—Fiction. | Magic—Fiction. | LCGFT: Fantasy fiction. | Light novels.
Classification: LCC PZ7.1.H3773 If 2023 | DDC [Fic]—dc23
LC record available at https://lccn.loc.gov/2023028673

ISBNs: 978-1-9753-7593-5 (paperback)
978-1-9753-7594-2 (ebook)

10 9 8 7 6 5 4 3 2 1

LSC-C

Printed in the United States of America

CHAPTER 1

The Flame of Love Burns Out

"Brigitte Meidell, I am officially breaking off our engagement!"

It happened in the middle of a party in the central hall of the school of magic.

When the crowd heard the Third Prince's outburst, everyone had the same reaction.

So it finally happened.

The gazes of the finely dressed youths gravitated toward one person. Needless to say, that person was the young lady the prince was addressing—Brigitte Meidell.

But the earl's daughter didn't even notice that everyone was staring at her. She simply stood there with her mouth hanging indecorously open.

Although her makeup was a bit heavy, she was a beautiful girl with fine features. Her bright red hair shimmered like raging flames, and sharp, intelligent eyes glinted like emeralds. Although the design of her lacy, beribboned pink dress was lovely enough, it was too childish to flatter her grown-up figure.

A boy and a girl were standing in front of her.

The boy was Brigitte's fiancé, Joseph Field, the Third Prince of the Kingdom of Field.

The girl was Lisa Selmin, a baron's daughter with the sort of pretty features that tended to arouse protective instincts.

The two of them were standing so close, they looked like a pair of mythological Chinese lovebirds joined at the breast…

With them glaring at her, Brigitte looked exactly like some storybook villainess. As the other students stared at this tableau, they realized something.

Joseph had rented out the hall for a party to celebrate the end of test season—but that was merely an excuse.

The real reason for inviting so many of their classmates to gather that day was simply to create a stage where Brigitte could be turned into a public laughingstock.

"But…why? Why, Your Highness?" Brigitte cried, her voice cracking from the shock.

Laughter bubbled up from the crowd of students.

Joseph frowned at her. He was known for his mild manners, but he answered her roughly—he must have been furious.

"I hardly think I need to tell you! I know how jealous you are of my dear friend Lisa. I know you've been secretly bullying her!"

A murmur ran through the crowd, drowning out Brigitte's wail ("I have not!").

Lisa's eyes teared up, as if she'd been waiting for this moment.

"It's been so awful, Miss Brigitte…and I haven't done anything wrong!"

As Lisa sobbed quietly, Joseph wrapped his arm protectively around her. Unlike Brigitte, Lisa looked perfect in her frilly pink dress. She gazed up at Joseph, blushing.

©Yomi Sarachi

This was the last straw for Brigitte. "But, but—Your Highness! I have no idea what she's talking about!" she cried desperately.

"It's far too late for you to play innocent!" he roared back.

"Do you have proof? Prove that I've been cruel to the baron's daughter!"

"I don't need proof! Lisa would never lie to me!"

Brigitte had nothing to say to that. Meanwhile, the other students began to fill in the silence with whispers.

"Imagine treating poor Lisa so viciously!"

"She thought she could do whatever she wanted because she was the prince's fiancée."

"The Red Fairy must be on fire with jealousy... How frightening..."

They were talking quietly, but not so quietly that Brigitte couldn't hear. No one was standing up for her.

After all, most people hated Brigitte Meidell. She was so worthless that she'd contracted with a no-name, and yet she'd been engaged to the Third Prince just because she was from a good family. She was haughty, domineering, and mean. If she was harassing a baron's daughter, too, then of course no one was going to defend her.

She heard all of it.

She must finally have realized that she didn't have a single friend in the crowd. Worse, even if she flew out of the hall, she wouldn't find a single friend in the entire land.

Everyone knew it, which was why the laughter swirling around her grew steadily louder. As she stared at the floor, her whole body shaking, Joseph jabbed his finger at her and delivered his verdict.

"Brigitte, I'll say this one more time. I am ending my engagement to you."

"..."

She couldn't even muster an answer now. Pale-faced, she gripped the hem of her skirt and managed to bow once. As she staggered toward the door, Joseph landed his final blow.

"Don't ever come near Lisa or me again!"

She paused very briefly, but then, as if to salvage a final shred of pride, she walked out of the hall without looking back.

It goes without saying that after that, the party came to life. The hall was buzzing with sneers and laughter until late that night, all at Brigitte's expense.

They were called the Fire Clan.

Skilled at fire magic and crowned with bright, burning red hair, the Meidells were a distinguished noble family who had earned their nickname long ago. Brigitte was the oldest daughter of the Earl of Meidell.

Ever since the Kingdom of Field was founded, the custom had been for all children to be taken to the shrine on their fifth birthday to enter into a contract with a spirit. Although the spirit world was, by nature, at odds with the human world, its inhabitants sometimes granted people the right to use a portion of their power. For example, if a contract was formed with a water spirit, the child could expect to be skilled at water magic. A contract with a wind spirit ensured skill in wind magic, and a contract with an earth spirit, skill in earth magic.

On the other hand, children not fortunate enough to have a spirit had no magical skill.

For both children and their parents, the contract ceremony held important meaning: It determined their future.

Like all the other children, Brigitte was taken to the shrine for the contracting ceremony on the day she turned five. It was eleven years ago now, but she remembered it as if it were yesterday. She would never forget it.

"...And the spirit contracted with the earl's daughter Bridget Meidell...is a no-name."

Embarrassment tinged the priest's voice as he made the announcement.

A loud buzz went through the crowd at the shrine. When little Brigitte turned fearfully around, she saw that the eager expectation on her parents' faces had vanished.

"No-name" was the common name for tiny spirits.

Tiny spirits were very weak, and while they did glow faintly, they couldn't even float. They were the dregs of the spirit world, not even worthy of individual spirit names among humans. That was why they were all placed under the label "no-name."

It wasn't unusual for commoners to contract with one of these. Some families were grateful to contract with any spirit at all. But for the oldest daughter of an earl, especially the bloodline of the Fire Clan—well, word of this unheard-of event spread like wildfire.

It must have come as quite a tragedy to little Brigitte when the very same year, the son of the Water Clan, a family often praised in the same breath as the Meidells, contracted with not one but two first-class spirits.

As soon as Brigitte returned to her family's mansion that day, her father grabbed her arm and thrust her left hand into the roaring hearth fire. She struggled to free herself, wailing from the heat and pain, but her father continued his terrifying punishment and refused to let anyone else in the household intervene. But after the priest who had been called to treat Brigitte's burn left, the Earl of Meidell insisted glumly that he was only trying to reset her contract.

"If this *thing* really is our child, she would never have contracted with a no-name. By making her touch the fire, I was only trying to find out if she was a changeling," he claimed.

Needless to say, Brigitte could not think of him as her father after that, and a blistered burn remained on the back of her left hand. The wound was so deep that even the high-ranking priest was unable to heal it fully. From then on, she hid her hands in gloves.

Many people believed the Earl of Meidell was in the right for this series of events, and they mocked Brigitte whenever they saw her. At tea parties and other social gatherings for the children of nobles, the others weren't ashamed to point at her and titter among themselves.

Before she knew it, people were calling the poor girl "the Red Fairy." Fairies were said to have less magical power than other spirits. All the children laughed and said it was perfect for a girl whose ability fell so short of her breeding.

One day, in the midst of this misery, Brigitte met someone at a tea party who changed her life.

Joseph, the Third Prince.

As she sat scowling in a corner, talking to no one, he came over along with his guard and casually struck up a conversation.

"Miss Brigitte, tell me what you like," he said as she sat tongue-tied before the handsome prince.

She blinked a few times, then said the first thing that came to mind: "I like spirits."

Instantly, she regretted answering so honestly.

People in the Kingdom of Field believed the old tales about changelings, the spirits who took the place of newborn babies, and several times a year, news of such an incident was reported. Although she was young, Brigitte knew well that one of the reasons people called her the Red Fairy was to suggest teasingly that the real Brigitte Meidell had been switched at birth with a red-haired fairy.

"Really? Why's that?" Joseph asked. He didn't sound like he was teasing her, which was a first for Brigitte. And so, despite the red rising in her cheeks, she was able to answer him with confidence.

"...Spirits can be frightening, but...I think they're very beautiful."

"Huh. Good answer."

That was all. That was how it began.

Joseph, the Third Prince, simply said those words and smiled. But to the young Brigitte, that reply saved her in ways she never could have imagined.

Joseph must have liked her, because the royal family sent an official notice, and soon after, the two were engaged.

Her parents cautiously sent a servant to tell her—she never saw them in person anymore. When she heard the news, she could have floated to the ceiling. Joseph was her only friend, and her attachment to him was hardly surprising.

But soon enough, even her savior began to change.

"My favorite girls are the stupid ones," he declared coldly one day.

Brigitte was confused. If he had a preference, she wanted to be the kind of fiancée he preferred, but she simply couldn't understand what he was saying.

"...What do you mean by stupid girls?" she asked hesitantly.

"Exactly."

"What?"

"Girls who don't know anything and want other people to tell them. Like you did just now. That's what I like."

Brigitte couldn't find a response, but Joseph's mood seemed to improve.

Things like this began happening every day.

"I like girls who look good in pink. I'll bet their brains are the exact same color."

"I'm bored; you should try ranting and raving a bit to make life more interesting."

"You should cover your face with makeup. Put it on so thick that no one can see what you look like without it."

"Nobody likes a girl who scores better on her tests than her fiancé. Hasn't that ever occurred to you?"

Brigitte was desperate—desperate to become whatever Joseph liked. She changed more and more about herself. She threw away all her favorite clothes. She filled her closet with an overflow of pink. She changed how she talked. She changed how she treated people, sneering at them until everyone hated her. She switched out all her makeup and started caking it on. She intentionally missed half the answers on her tests. She threw away her old self and became someone new.

After all...

I want His Highness to think I'm cute.

Yes, at the start, she was sure she had felt a weak kind of love.

But what about now?

She tried to think on it, but she couldn't make sense of anything. His eyes had been so kind back when they had first met, but that was a thing of the past. Now all she saw was a mix of contempt and hatred—no one would normally act this way toward the fiancée they had chosen for themselves.

Although I don't need to worry about that anymore...

She was frustrated with herself for even now trying to rethink the situation.

It was all over.

He broke our engagement...

She couldn't help remembering the previous night's party.

She lay on her bed with her arms wrapped around her knees and squeezed her eyes shut.

At least she didn't have school today. There was no way she could have dragged herself to class.

The scene outside her window was sodden with the rain that had been falling since morning.

She slipped in and out of wakefulness, but she found no peace. Maybe it was the incessant sound of the rain.

The day her father had burned her hand when she was five—

A light rain had started in the morning, too. Her left hand began to twitch, and she pressed it with her right.

It hurts...

She had been dragged into the drawing room.

She remembered the iron grip of her father as she stood before the blazing hearth.

Her throat had tightened with terror, but she was no match for the strength in a man's large hand.

In her memories, her father took the form of a devil berating her again and again. He shouted and shoved her hand into the flames while she screamed.

"Can't you do something right for once in your life, you worthless excuse for a child—?"

Brigitte squeezed her eyes shut and covered her ears, trying not to hear his voice.

It's been eleven years, but...

Why did it still hurt so much? She grimaced.

At the sound of a knock on the door, she hurriedly lifted her face and answered awkwardly.

Sienna, her waiting maid, stepped into the room. "Miss Brigitte," she said, her angled orange bob falling forward over her uniform as she bowed her head.

Sienna was two years older than Brigitte, a merchant's daughter distantly related to the Meidells. She was short and appeared much younger than Brigitte when the two stood next to each other, but she was very competent, and Brigitte not only trusted her completely but secretly admired her as well.

"I brought you something easy to digest. Please try to eat a little."

She kneeled next to the bed and peered into Brigitte's face. When their eyes met, Brigitte thought she caught a shade of pain in Sienna's expression. Sienna was always beautiful and dignified, but there was an urgency in her voice. She was clearly worried about her mistress.

The previous night when Brigitte came home, she had said she wasn't feeling well, and she hadn't left her room since.

Everyone knows what happened...

Joseph had ended their engagement.

He had accused her of things she had no recollection of doing, berated her for them...and she had crawled home like she was running from him.

There was no way her parents hadn't heard. But no one asked her about it. She didn't even know if they were relieved or disappointed.

"If I weren't your waiting maid...I'd give you a hug to cheer you up."

"No one would blame you if you did."

Sienna stood up and timidly wrapped her arms around Brigitte.

"You've been suffering for more than a decade... I'm so sorry I couldn't do anything to help you."

"What are you talking about? You've always been so thoughtful. I'm sorry," Brigitte answered.

Sienna stiffened in surprise. "No," she said, her voice unsteady.

Brigitte wondered why she hadn't apologized sooner and wished she had.

All the maids in the cottage, not just Sienna, had hinted at how she should handle Joseph and his constant demands.

I was so stupid... I didn't listen to a word they said...

Brigitte and Sienna hadn't always gotten along well. It had to do with the fact that the whole reason the Meidell cottage had been built was to isolate Brigitte.

I feel so bad for them. I was the one being punished, but they had to suffer along with me. They didn't do anything wrong...

Brigitte's father had not been able to forgive her for contracting with a no-name spirit. He declared she had no right to live in the main Meidell residence and hastily ordered a cottage built in a far corner of the estate. It was there that he moved the five-year-old Brigitte, who was still recovering from her burns.

He had told her never to show her face in the manor again and called her a blemish on the Meidell name.

Brigitte's mother refused to look her in the eye, as if the little girl had become a monstrosity to her.

The earl ordered Sienna and several other maids to care for Brigitte, forcing them out of the main residence. Cooks and gardeners, too. Those judged unfit for service in the main house were transferred with Brigitte to the cottage.

For this reason, relations between Brigitte and her staff in the early days were less than ideal. But after years of seeing her every day, they seemed to have warmed to her. They did not give up on her even when she went out and played the arrogant lady Joseph wanted her to be.

The only reason she survived her isolation after her family's rejection, and the only reason she wasn't giving in to despair after her fiancé's rejection, was because Sienna and the other servants had stayed by her side. Here in this cramped cage, their presence was the only warmth she knew.

…She's so toasty.

Thanks to Sienna's arms around her, she felt a hint of warmth return to her frozen body.

"…Thank you, Sienna," she murmured.

Sienna slowly released her. Her orange eyes glinted with mischief, which was unusual.

"When the rain stops…," she began.

"Yes?"

"Let's burn your pink dresses."

"What? But—"

"Let's burn them all. How does that sound?" Sienna said, smiling slightly.

Brigitte nodded under the influence of her waiting maid's quiet power.

"Anyhow, the cook made you some warm stew, so I hope you'll have a bowl. The head chef is so worried about you, he's wandering around the kitchen with his knife in his hand."

"Th-that doesn't sound good… All right, I'll have some. You'd better hurry and tell Nathan that I'm going to eat it."

One of the advantages of the cottage was that the cook was always ready to serve her a warm meal, and it was always just the right amount.

Looking satisfied by Brigitte's flustered answer, Sienna nodded and said, "I'll tell him. Shall I bring it to your room?"

"Yes, if you don't mind."

"I'll bring it right away," Sienna said politely.

Brigitte felt like it had been ages since they'd had an ordinary exchange like this.

"...I don't see what about you is arrogant or foolish, Miss Brigitte Meidell," Sienna murmured.

By the time Brigitte realized what she'd said, Sienna had disappeared out the door.

CHAPTER 2

A Chance Encounter Between Birds of a Feather

Two days had passed since Joseph broke off the engagement. As Brigitte walked down the hallway on her way to class in another building, she could feel people staring at her... It was incredibly awkward.

It's like every person in this school knows what happened...

Still, she didn't let it show on her face, throwing her shoulders back as she walked. No matter what they said or how much they laughed, she was determined not to let them get the best of her.

That was her sole wish...but the truth was, she already felt discouraged.

What in the world do I do now?

Seemingly overnight, she had tumbled from her position as the prince's fiancée to just another discarded adolescent girl.

Suddenly, as she turned the corner of the hallway, something knocked her shoulder, and she tottered slightly. She'd bumped into a male student walking toward her. But before she could stop herself, she was already snapping at him.

"How rude! You should look where you're walking!"

She glared at him. The boy's face twitched, but he said nothing and simply ran away down the hall.

I have to stop acting this way! Why am I always saying such things?

Her eyes grew hot. But if she cried, she knew people would laugh at her even more. So she bit her lip and blinked back the tears.

She couldn't remember when, exactly, Joseph had told her he liked haughty, domineering girls. To please him, she had cast aside her timid, quiet self in favor of an arrogant, cruel personality that took advantage of her position as the prince's fiancée. Soon the unwanted nickname the Red Fairy became even more firmly attached to her.

Just now, she really had wanted to apologize.

"...Arghhh," she sighed.

How silly is it that I can't even speak normally anymore?

She was able to stay calmer when she was talking to one of the kind cottage servants. She knew she couldn't go on like this, but getting rid of ingrained habits wasn't easy.

She glanced up and noticed that sunbeams were pouring through the school windows. But even with the clear blue sky, so bright it stung her eyes, her dark mood refused to lighten. Plus, she hated to see the gaudy reflection of her made-up face in the window.

"Did you hear me, Yuri Aurealis?"

Brigitte froze at the sound of the voice ahead of her. She knew she didn't need to hide...but she slipped behind a pillar anyway. When she timidly peeked out, she saw the backs of two familiar figures just down the hallway.

Joseph and Lisa.

The humiliation and sadness of two days earlier flooded back, and she squeezed her fists in front of her chest.

There was a boy standing in front of them, too. "Of course. I've been listening to you this whole time, Prince Joseph," he said.

"...How dare you speak so rudely to royalty?"

Brigitte recognized the boy. There probably wasn't a student in school who didn't know his name—Yuri Aurealis. He was possibly even more famous than Joseph, the Third Prince.

The son of the Water Clan...

The House of Aurealis was a prominent dukedom, and many of its members were skilled at water magic. Their lineage was impeccable.

Brigitte had met Yuri several times, but she had never had a real conversation with him. Still, she was extremely aware of him.

Perhaps that was because so many people mentioned the House of Meidell and the House of Aurealis in the same breath. One was skilled at fire magic and the other at water magic, and serendipitously, many children were born with red hair in the one and blue hair in the other.

However, in contrast to the tiny spirit Brigitte had contracted with, Yuri had contracted with not one but two first-class spirits, despite being the duke's fourth son. He was a genius without equal.

As was common among those with excellent magic lineage, in both the Meidell and Aurealis families, only legitimate sons or daughters who contracted with a first-class spirit were qualified to take on the family title. Rumor had it that Yuri would certainly inherit the title of duke in his family. Although his eldest brother had also contracted with a powerful spirit, Yuri was so incredibly talented that his older brother was scarcely mentioned.

Yuri had a reputation for treating everyone with cold cruelty. And sure enough, at this very moment, he was looking at Joseph and Lisa without a hint of warmth in his eyes. The rumors about the dozens of girls he'd rejected probably weren't lies, either. Thanks to his personality and his extraordinary abilities, people called him the Frozen Blade.

People hate him just as much as they hate me...

That was probably the only thing they had in common.

Of course, in Brigitte's case, the hatred came from contempt, while in Yuri's case, it probably came from jealousy and desire for what he had.

Right now, Joseph seemed to be lashing out at the duke's son.

"Then apologize to Lisa. You should be able to do that, I believe?"

"...I cannot consent to that, Your Highness."

With his blue-black hair and foxlike yellow eyes, which were especially sharp at the moment, Yuri was stunningly attractive. He wasn't especially tall, and his pale skin and delicate features made him look almost like a girl at first glance. Still, as Brigitte peeked out from her hiding spot, she felt overwhelmed by his power. Was it the indifference in his gaze that made her feel this way? He could cut someone in half with that look.

"I did not go out of my way to treat Baron Selmin's daughter poorly. If I had to say one way or the other, I'd say I treat everyone the same as I treat her."

"You're an obnoxiously brazen person, you know that? Lisa is a close friend of mine, and I am royalty!"

"And how, exactly, does that relate to me?"

Yuri frowned, looking bored, while Joseph growled angrily.

But Brigitte already understood the situation, by and large. She let out a muffled sigh.

Joseph is angry with him for how he treated Lisa...

...How ridiculous. She wondered if Joseph would go on threatening anyone who didn't please him. Just like he'd assumed that she'd been bullying Lisa and passed judgment on her. What in the world had happened to the kind, thoughtful Joseph she'd first met?

As she thought about all of this…her eyes met Yuri's over Joseph's shoulder. She froze, then frantically retracted her neck.

Did he see me?

If word got out that she was eavesdropping, it would be more than a little bad for her reputation. She tiptoed away from her hiding spot. Behind her, she could still hear Joseph yelling. A crowd seemed to be gathering.

Yuri was probably about to be publicly disgraced just like she had been. But even as the thought crossed her mind, she realized he wasn't likely to become the butt of everyone's jokes the way she had. No matter what Joseph said to him, he held his ground.

He's cold and blunt and unpleasant…

She knew that.

But secretly, she was just a tiny bit impressed by his prickliness.

After school that day, Brigitte headed to the library. The truth was, although she was in the lower half of her class, she wasn't naturally bad at reading or studying. In fact, she enjoyed those things. Everyone thought her head was full of rocks, but storybooks and textbooks didn't care who turned their pages.

Joseph…I mean, His Highness used to tell me a library wasn't a place for dumb girls to hang out, she thought, correcting herself midsentence. *But I'm not his fiancée anymore, so I can do what I want, can't I?*

The school she attended in the woods outside the capital of the Kingdom of Field was called the Otoleanna Academy of Magic. On the right side of the formidable stone school was the Magical Experiment Building, and behind that was the library. The shelves of the sprawling brick building overflowed with books on wizardry and history that never made it into the textbooks.

Now that she had lost Joseph's support—if she could call it that, or maybe *protection* was a better word—Brigitte knew she would have to look out for herself. Her adopted brother was to take over the Meidell family title. He was a distant relation of the Meidells whom her father had adopted because he was contracted with a first-class spirit. Shut away in the cottage, Brigitte had hardly even met him. Although he should have been a year behind her in school, she had never seen him at the academy. She assumed he had been forbidden from interacting with her.

It's not that I have anything against him...

But as long as he was there, Brigitte wasn't needed. She knew it was highly likely that in the not-so-distant future, she would be cast out of her home. And because she knew that, she also knew she couldn't let herself be swept away by her reputation as a selfish, arrogant person.

Witnessing Yuri that afternoon was probably what put the thought in her mind. Something had struck her powerfully as she watched him.

I have to get myself back.

She couldn't exactly put it into words, but that was how she felt. Her real self. She had to follow her heart.

I think I'll stop putting my makeup on so heavy, she suddenly thought, touching the pancaked foundation on her cheek. Sienna and the other maids would probably cry with joy when she told them. They had always insisted that she had naturally strong features, which simple makeup would suit better. She was the one who had ignored them and done as Joseph wished.

It's not only the cosmetics. It's how I talk...how I laugh...

It was terrible of her to have been so haughty.

She was embarrassed to think of how she used to hold her fan and laugh so loudly.

She hated those showy pink dresses; if only she could wear elegantly simple clothing.

She knew many people thought poorly of her now. She could change that little by little, as long as she was moving forward, but...

The first step is to start speaking normally.

This is going to be a long journey, she thought glumly as she walked. She had arrived at the library without even realizing it. The building was surprisingly empty, even though many intellectuals came from outside the school to use it.

The librarians at the front desk looked shocked when she walked in...but when she bowed her head, they bowed timidly back. Still, they didn't exactly show any desire to talk to her. She found a map of the library and decided to seek out what she needed on her own.

Now, where is it...? Aha! Here!

Hugging a thick, old book to her chest, she walked to a seat. The large reading area was completely empty. She'd planned to check the book out but decided she might as well read it there.

It was called the *Illustrated Encyclopedia of Spirits.*

Their world was home to spirits of every variety. Although many mysteries remained about these creatures, who normally did as they pleased in their home realm, those who contracted with humans were pictured in the book along with various facts about them.

Since the most powerful spirits—like an ifrit, the spirit her father was contracted with—could speak human language fluently, the encyclopedia began with descriptions of the customs in the spirit world and illustrations of its landscapes that were supposedly based on their accounts.

Brigitte loved spirits and the colorful world they inhabited. She couldn't help smiling like a child whenever she read about them.

...Of course, she had no idea how much of that delight was showing on her face.

The waterfall is not spanned by a rainbow; rather, the water itself is rainbow-colored. Those who are charmed by its beauty and drink the water typically experience nausea, so care should be taken.

She was so absorbed by the two-page spreads of fantastical scenes that she forgot to blink.

Fire spirits breathed out sparks, water spirits breathed out mud, wind spirits breathed out air. Light spirits breathed out stored-up light, and everything around them shone so bright that night never came. If one could entice a light spirit to drink a rainbow for a party, that party would be truly magical.

If you pound hard on rocky ground, little spirits who had been idling the time away will come tumbling out... What's this? If someone sneezes, heaven and earth switch places? How funny...

Brigitte couldn't help giggling at how fun and free the life of spirits seemed. As she turned the next page, she happened to look up—and couldn't believe her eyes.

...*Yuri Aurealis?*

How long had he been there?

He was sitting two rows away from her with his chin resting on one hand. Lit up by the sun from the window as he read the book in his other hand, he was as beautiful as a picture. Just before she lost herself completely in this vision, he raised his head. Flustered, she looked back down at the encyclopedia.

Yuri was far ahead of his classmates both in classroom studies and practical skills, so it wasn't surprising that he was in the library.

But Brigitte felt guilty for having spied on him while Joseph was yelling at him a few hours earlier.

But it would be awkward to apologize now...

She decided to go on reading as if nothing had happened.

The same thing occurred the next day.

And the day after that.

As Brigitte was reading, Yuri would appear and silently begin reading his own books. Or sometimes, she would arrive quietly after he was already there. She always sat in the same place, and his regular seat appeared to be two rows ahead of hers. He paid no attention to her. She didn't even know if he noticed her. After so many years where attention from others meant mockery would soon follow, this was a relief.

One day, however, the routine changed.

"Oh!"

"..."

Brigitte reached out for a book and accidentally touched Yuri's hand. Their fingertips brushed, and their eyes met.

I've read about such things in romance novels...

Her heart was beating a tiny bit faster than usual. Up close, his deep yellow eyes shone like citrine. She could see herself reflected in them, mouth agape...

Before she could think, she was speaking.

"...Would you mind moving your hand? I got here first."

A few seconds after making this brusque request, she felt the blood drain from her face.

Now I've d-done it...!

It was true that old habits were hard to break...but that was an incredibly rude thing to say to a duke's son. Still, his expression remained blank.

"...You want to read this, too?" he asked flatly.

Brigitte blinked at this unexpected question. She had heard he was cold and cruel, but if he didn't blame her for talking to him like that, did that mean he was also forgiving?

"Um, yes, I do."

"Oh."

In the instant when her guard was down, his hand shot out and snatched the book from the shelf.

"Ah!"

She didn't even have time to protest. Without a backward glance, he returned to his usual seat and began reading as if nothing was amiss. All Brigitte could do was reel from shock.

...What just happened?!

Who talked to people to distract them, then mercilessly stole their book? What an outrageous thing for a high-class noble to do! Even as she fumed, however, she had to admit that she had been equally rude.

Grumbling resentfully, she chose another book and returned to her seat. She set it upright on the long desk and glared furtively over the top... Yuri was coolly flipping the pages of his book, chin in hand.

Disgusted, she attempted to concentrate on her own reading.

...Perhaps it was only natural that her irritation grew stronger instead, until she found it impossible to focus.

Perhaps I'll just check this one out and leave...

She sighed, just as a shadow fell over her head. Puzzled, she looked up.

"Hey."

"...Ah?!"

Yuri was standing next to her. Brigitte stiffened.

What's he about to do? Hit me?!

As she tensed defensively, he held something out, and her gaze fell to the book they had both wanted. A beautiful wind spirit engraved on the old leather cover smiled up at her.

"I've already memorized what I need from this."

When the meaning of his words registered, she could find no words to reply. He was genuinely saying he didn't want it anymore.

Could that be why he took it in the first place...?

Maybe it was wishful thinking on her part. But maybe he was kinder than the rumors made him out to be, after all. She felt more confused than ever.

He said he memorized it...but it's hundreds of pages!

"Th-thank y—"

"You know about this book?" he asked, arms crossed as he interrupted her awkward thank-you.

She nodded vaguely, absorbed by his appearance.

"Huh? Oh, I suppose—"

"That's a surprise."

Click.

Instantly, an awful sound echoed in her head.

He's making fun of me.

She couldn't keep quiet if that was the case. In the past, she'd always responded to any insult with a haughty laugh. But she didn't want to be that person anymore. She stood quietly and pointed to the book's cover.

"This is an original copy of *The Wind Laughs*, I believe."

"It is. And?"

So what? he was saying.

She spoke a bit louder to avoid being overwhelmed. "The author of *The Wind Laughs* is the late Lien Baluanuki, a well-known scholar of spirits. Although Lien himself contracted with a third-class spirit, he became close with the sylphide a friend had contracted with and is rumored to have spoken frequently with her."

"..."

"This book is said to be based on what the sylphide told him about the spirit world. It became famous overnight for its unique depiction of subjects beyond human knowledge and because it was written in spirit language. Translators vary greatly in their interpretations, but the consensus is that it is a book of many mysteries to which no conclusive answer has yet been found.

"Based on the fact that the sylphide taught Lien her language, some scholars have argued that the two were lovers, or else as close as family. Some call the book Lien's love letter to the spirits. As a reader, however, I prefer not to cheapen their relationship with such descriptions."

After reeling off her explanation, Brigitte noticed a hint of surprise on Yuri's face.

"Are you really the Earl of Meidell's daughter?"

"I am. I should have introduced myself sooner. My name is Brigitte Meidell."

Pleased at having outwitted him, she dipped her head elegantly.

Yuri rested his hand on his chin in thought. After a few moments of silence, she began to wonder what he was going to say.

"...How strange. I heard the Third Prince's fiancée was a stupid, out-of-control terror."

"Wh—?"

"Oh, excuse me. Now that you're no longer engaged, I should have said a stupid, ordinary redhead."

"Wha-wha-wha-what?"

Brigitte flushed bright red at this outrageous insult.

How dare he say that to my face!

The terrifying thing was, he was saying it so calmly that she didn't sense any malice. She squeezed her fists under the desk. What a ludicrous person this Yuri Aurealis was!

"Um, excuse me, but would you mind keeping your voice down in the library?"

Just then, a female librarian approached them fearfully. Brigitte had heard that many of the library staff were commoners. She could imagine how frightening it must be to approach such a universally hated pair as Yuri and herself. She felt guilty, but Yuri just glanced at the librarian and said, "Sorry. I'll make sure to remind her to keep quiet."

Hey, don't blame this on me!

It was Yuri's fault that she'd raised her voice, and he was the one who had started talking to her in the first place. He was in the wrong, but he was acting as if she had annoyed *him*.

"Speaking in a loud voice at the library is against the rules," he said. "Of course, it's even worse to go around spewing insignificant facts like you were doing just now. You ought to be more thoughtful of those around you!"

Snap.

She heard a sound somewhere in her head.

She smiled brightly, although veins were bulging at her temples.

"...Mr. Aurealis, may I have a word in private?"

"You think I have time to waste on you?"

"It will only take a moment."

"..."

Perhaps realizing that Brigitte was not going to back down, Yuri sighed with irritation.

Brigitte dragged the reluctant Yuri to a garden across the street from one side of the library. They walked down a stone path in the meticulously maintained garden to a small gazebo next to a staircase. Brigitte sat first, and Yuri sat across from her with obvious displeasure. She glared straight at his perfect face. No one could complain if she yelled at him out here.

"I want to tell you, Mr. Aurealis—," she began.

"What?" he interrupted.

"It's not wise to call a stupid person stupid."

Yuri blinked at her.

She continued her unremitting sermon.

"I read once in a book that doing so only makes their foolishness worse."

"..."

"It's been said since ancient times that spirits dwell in words. Think of magic. Nothing happens without a spell, right?"

"I can do magic without spells."

Oh, shut up!

Not everyone was a genius like he was. Using himself as the standard hardly made sense.

"What I mean is—I would like for you to stop calling me stupid!" she said resolutely.

He was silent for a moment. A breeze blew past them.

Without taking her eyes off Yuri, she tucked an unruly strand of hair behind her ear.

"...I never called you stupid," he muttered.

You didn't?

She believed he'd called her stupid quite a few times.

"I heard that you were a stupid, out-of-control girl without a shred of intelligence. But you've read the original edition of *The Wind Laughs* and lots of other things, too...so I was just thinking that you can't trust rumors."

He stared straight at her.

"Were you pretending to be a fool?"

He'd guessed the truth.

He must have taken her quiet panic as affirmation, because he frowned and asked, "Why?" He sounded genuinely bewildered.

"..."

Brigitte was having a hard time answering. She'd been too wrapped up in scolding him to notice before, but it was more than a little unnerving being stared at by a boy beautiful enough to be a statue in the sunlight. And on top of that, for some reason, he was asking about personal things.

I thought the Frozen Blade wasn't interested in other people...

Maybe that explained what happened next.

"...You m-might not believe this, but I used to be a shy, timid little girl..."

Before she knew it, she found herself telling him things about her past that she hadn't planned on ever sharing with anyone.

Falteringly, Brigitte told him the story of her life from early childhood through the present—although she left out the part about the rift with her parents. He wouldn't enjoy hearing that.

Yuri listened quietly, hardly even offering the usual *ahs* or *ohs*. Maybe that was why she was able to speak reasonably calmly and not lose her thread. When she finally ended her story with the broken engagement, Yuri asked, "Are you stupid?"

He said it again!

She almost flopped face down on the table from shock. But Yuri kept gazing at her, arms crossed, as if she were some incomprehensible creature.

"What is the point of changing your makeup, your clothes, your speech, and even your personality just because your fiancé told you to?"

He had a point. She didn't have a good answer, but she mumbled, "I only... That's what happens when you like someone."

She knew it was a pitiful answer. Her eyes burned, and her voice was shaking.

It was true that she'd liked Joseph. She wanted to be the kind of girl he liked, too. She wanted him to think she was cute. She had devoted eleven years of her life to that wish. She realized now that it had all been pointless—but she didn't want to reject the part of herself that had worked so hard.

"If it would win his love, I was ready and willing to do idiotic things that no one else could understand... Of course, when I think about it now, I can see how silly it was."

Clearly uninterested in love affairs, Yuri eyed her coldly.

"Huh," he said—though strangely enough, his tone was kind.

Brigitte looked up, but he wasn't gazing at her. His attention was on some point in the distance.

"I don't really understand it...but Joseph was lucky to be loved by you."

"...!"

His words cut straight to her core. She stared at him wide-eyed.

I never thought I'd hear anyone say something so kind to me.

His fairy-tale words spread through her heart. He hadn't said them for Joseph. He had said them for her.

I feel like all my hard work has been rewarded.

"But don't you think that's just an excuse?"

"...What?"

She abruptly returned from deep, moist-eyed emotion to real life. She had completely let her guard down.

After all, she was sitting across from the Frozen Blade—the duke's son who was rumored to lack both blood and tears.

"I mean, haven't you ever suspected that you're blaming your own lack of intelligence on infatuation?"

"What?!"

What is "lack of intelligence" supposed to mean?!

Who the hell did he think he was?

She banged the table and stood up. "You have some nerve, Mr. Aurealis! How dare you speak so rudely to a girl in love!"

"Oh, be quiet. Your voice is piercing."

"And whose fault is that?!"

It didn't help that he was plugging his ears irritably.

"If you must know, I was often called a genius when I was a baby!"

"Stupid parents tend to say that. Mine said the same thing."

Her patience finally snapped at Yuri's spiteful words. Without waiting to calm down, she growled, "...Then the game is on, Mr. Aurealis."

"What game?"

"In our next written exams...let's see who gets the higher score."

Yuri stared back at her in confusion.

"I've gotten the top score on every test since I started here," he said.

"...I am aware of that. But I do not plan to lose to you," Brigitte said, her emerald eyes burning.

Yuri narrowed his strangely wintry citrine eyes. He stood and smiled at her like a storybook villain.

"Fine. Challenge accepted."

Brigitte was surprised. Was Yuri secretly a sore loser?

"If this is a game, then wouldn't it be fun to have a prize?"

Brigitte hadn't considered this. She rested a finger on her chin and looked up at the gazebo's roof.

©Yomi Sarashi

"That's true. It's a cliché, but let's say the loser has to do one thing the winner says, whatever it is."

"Agreed."

She had suggested it casually, but he took the bait without missing a beat. She panicked. In retrospect, her actions and words had been full of mistakes. For instance, speaking disrespectfully to a duke's son. She wasn't backing down, but she was feeling increasingly anxious.

This might cost me...

"Can we say that it can't be anything violent...?" she asked.

"Just what kind of person do you think I am?" he snapped back. Brigitte nodded, even though she was uncertain.

I can only trust him...

And that was how the one-on-one competition between the villainess despised for her incompetence and the villain shunned for his intellect began.

You're kidding me!

As soon as Lisa poked her head into the classroom next to hers, she giggled. There was Brigitte Meidell—the girl who just days earlier had been dumped by her fiancé.

Given how haughty Brigitte was, Lisa had assumed she must spend her time in class shrieking miserably in that shrill voice of hers.

But she was wrong. A scene beyond even her active imagination was playing out before her eyes.

Brigitte was sitting at her desk next to the window in the back of the room. The desk was crowded with textbooks and reference books, which Brigitte was poring over while her right hand was busy taking down notes. It was obvious what this meant.

Could she be...studying? That idiot...?

It was so ridiculous, Lisa almost burst out laughing. Did she really think she could stuff anything into that empty head of hers if she started now? Or maybe she was too stupid to care what anyone else thought about her.

If she's trying to show everyone she's fine, that's even funnier.

The other students were clearly avoiding her. But Brigitte pretended not to hear them, apparently wrapped up in her studying.

No wonder Joseph dumped her...

As she silently mocked Brigitte, Lisa thought back on how she had met Joseph—the fiancé she stole from Brigitte.

To Lisa, the Third Prince Joseph Field was like a perfect storybook prince. He had shining golden hair and eyes the same color. He was tall, with the elegant, distinguished bearing befitting a royal. All the girls in school swooned over his handsome face and gentle smile.

Fortunately for Lisa, Joseph was in the same class as her. When she saw the list of names on the bulletin board, she could have leaped with joy. It was like a dream. She had suddenly stepped close to a fairy-tale character she had never expected to meet.

But the gap between Joseph, a prince, and herself, a mere baron's daughter, was wider than she'd realized. She didn't have a single chance to speak to him.

The turning point finally came half a year after starting at the academy, in a medicinal herbology class. She had been placed in the same group as him, which was exciting enough...but then, when they were gathering herbs outside, she happened to overhear Joseph muttering about a plant.

"What is this…?"

She recognized what was in his hand. It grew all over her family's domain. She walked up to him and told him the name and species; she had picked up a smattering of knowledge from her family gardener a few years back.

She was so nervous, she hardly remembered what she had said…but when she was done, Joseph smiled kindly at her.

"You're very smart, Miss Selmin."

"Really…?"

Lisa thought her ears were playing tricks, while Joseph frowned as if something was troubling him.

"You're so different from my fiancée," he said.

Only then did she blush, because she realized he was praising her.

So the rumors about Prince Joseph hating his fiancée are true…

Lisa knew all about Joseph's fiancée and her awful reputation. She was a shameless girl who coasted on her status as the prince's intended and behaved in ways unfitting of a noble. But Joseph had been kind enough to stay by her side until now. It was a fable familiar to everyone in the land.

Apparently, though, even Joseph had finally had enough. Really, Joseph and Lisa's meeting must have been divinely fated.

Gradually, she and Joseph began to talk more often. Which isn't to say she was able to approach him whenever she wanted—he was still a prince, of course. But he started taking notice of her. And she always worried about him when he looked tired. She cursed Brigitte and praised him for putting up with her bad behavior. Her feelings must have reached him because he opened up to her…and eventually, they overcame the obstacles to be together.

Bored of staring at Brigitte, Lisa returned to her classroom. "Prince Joseph!" She ran up to the Third Prince just as he rose from his seat. She started to embrace him, not caring who saw, but he placed a gentle hand on her shoulder.

When she looked up in confusion, he whispered, "People might get in the way here. Let's go somewhere else."

"Oh, of course," she said, blushing like an innocent maiden as she left the room with him. Their classmates watched her enviously. She loved how it felt when every single person they passed in the hallway turned around to watch them. She kept her steps slow, her beautiful tresses flowing behind her, as she bathed in the attention of the masses.

Everything was so different from when she was just a dull baron's daughter. She never imagined a day would come when so many people wished they could be her, the girl the prince had fallen for. She was surrounded by a clique that constantly fussed over her. Even though Brigitte was an earl's daughter, Joseph had chosen Lisa instead.

True, Brigitte was pretty enough—but now she was no more than a miserable prop to enhance Lisa's story.

Brigitte Meidell, I hope you continue flailing in humiliation forever. Lisa giggled to herself.

"Prince Joseph, Brigitte is acting strange," she said as soon as they were alone in an empty classroom.

Joseph, who had walked in ahead of her, looked back. "...Did you go to see her?"

"Yes. I felt sorry for her. She was sitting at her desk writing something very seriously."

She couldn't help giggling, but Joseph raised his eyebrows. "Brigitte was studying?"

"Yes, it's strange, isn't it? It's futile for a girl so stupid."

"..."

Joseph suddenly fell quiet, but Lisa didn't think too much about it. He must be tired of seeing his ex-fiancée make such a fool of herself. That thought made her even happier, and she went on excitedly.

"I mean, in the last written tests, I heard she got one of the lowest scores of anyone. I'm sure she'll do even worse this time!"

"Ha-ha, I bet. Speaking of tests, you tend to struggle with written exams yourself, don't you?"

"Uh…!"

Lisa blushed at his question. He was right—Lisa's scores were usually closer to the bottom than the top. Still, she was far above Brigitte. That was why she'd been laughing.

But…

What if?

This was purely hypothetical, of course…but what if Brigitte threw herself into her studies and miraculously scored better than Lisa on the tests? Joseph would be disappointed. Lisa couldn't stand the thought of it.

I should do whatever I can to prevent that…

Who cared if she was being paranoid? Either way, she'd be able to make Brigitte's life more miserable.

Suddenly, as Lisa was scheming about how to harass Brigitte, Joseph wrapped her in a strong embrace.

"Ah…" She sighed from within his arms.

She was probably the only one who knew how forceful he could be. Her eyes closed in happiness at the thought.

After a few moments of bliss, she looked up at him, her heart pounding.

"Your Highness…I was wondering, when should we get engaged?"

"What?"

He tilted his head.

Lisa let her eyes grow moist. "I mean…I'd like to tell my parents soon."

"…I know, but think of appearances. It doesn't look very good to end one engagement and begin another right away. I think we should wait until the rumors die down."

Lisa felt more than a little sullen about his answer, but the only emotion she let show was sadness.

I suppose it can't be helped…but I want to act like the prince's official fiancée as soon as possible.

"Of course, I want to get engaged soon, too, Lisa."

"Oh, Your Highness…"

Cheered up by his words, she snuggled closer to him. He smiled, his arms around her waist, and Lisa savored the moment.

How divine… To think I'll be married to such a wonderful prince…

As she basked in this little sliver of paradise, Lisa didn't notice.

The look on his face when she'd mentioned their engagement wasn't a lovestruck daze—it was the empty stare of someone who didn't have a clue what he was being asked.

"…Now, Brigitte, why weren't you able to try harder?"

Little Brigitte was shivering. She couldn't stop, even in her mother's arms.

Although her mother's tone was kind, the words themselves held no mercy. Tears poured from Brigitte's eyes, but her mother did not relent. She sighed with pity, stared intently at Brigitte's bandaged hand, and repeated the same thing yet again.

"Your father is an illustrious man, contracted with an ifrit. Your uncle, too. The same has always been true for the House of Meidell…

except for you. Why are you the only one who couldn't do it? Did…I do something wrong? Is this my fault?"

"I'm sorry, Mommy, I'm sorry."

Brigitte apologized desperately. Her voice was nearly a whisper. Her head was so full of fear and anxiety and guilt toward her mother, she could hardly speak, while her mother watched her with hollow eyes.

"He's been saying unbelievable things—that you're someone else's child, or else a changeling. I have to agree that this scraggly red hair can't come from him. I never even wanted to marry into such a violent, fiery family…"

I'm sorry, Mommy, but I…

"Hey. Are you all right?"

For a moment after waking up, Brigitte couldn't answer. She had goose bumps all over her body and cold sweat on her cheeks. Trying to cover it up, she licked her dry lips. "…Yes, I'm fine."

She could hardly hear her own cracked voice. She didn't know when she'd fallen asleep, but here Yuri Aurealis was, standing in front of her with his well-shaped eyebrows knit together.

"You don't look fine."

When Brigitte had arrived at the library, there was a handful of other people there, but now the two of them appeared to be the only ones in the study area. She glanced out the window. The sky was already dim, so she must have been asleep for an hour or more. Yuri would have been studying in the quiet library, too. He had probably been annoyed by the sight of her sleeping and had come over to scold her.

"…I'm sorry. I can't believe I fell asleep here."

"Looks more like you passed out."

Brigitte didn't know what to say. Her fingers tightened around her pen. Her rivalry with Yuri was the reason she was losing sleep to study in the first place.

They were competing for the top score in the exams three weeks from now—and whoever lost would have to do one thing the other person told them to, whatever it was. It wasn't that she had some specific request in mind, since she hardly even knew Yuri, but she wanted revenge for all the times he'd called her stupid.

She didn't mind studying. She spent her days off reading school-books and other things anyway. She had bad grades, but that was only because she'd been trying to please Joseph.

Of course, I don't get much help from the spirits, so I really am awful at practical subjects...

For the past few days, she'd even been studying in class during breaks, with her texts and notebooks spread all over her desk. Whenever she had a question, she asked the teacher. She heard the other students laughing at her and calling her crazy, and one day she spotted Lisa smirking at her from the hallway...but she couldn't care less. She was burning to beat Yuri, and all the rest was noise.

And I have a dream.

She'd had it since she was young, but it had been a long time since she'd said it out loud. All her studying was for the achievement of that dream. That was why she never took the easy road.

...But whenever she thought about it, she wondered if the dream itself was a betrayal of her mother.

Because she wasn't contracted with a first-class spirit, Brigitte could not inherit her father's title. She was certain that in the future, she would not be allowed to keep her name on the family register. Working hard now so she'd be able to support herself in the future was a sensible thing to do.

Still.

Even now, she felt her mother's cold embrace around her, trapping her. As a shiver ran down her back, she heard Yuri's flat voice above her head.

"So, do you want to surrender while you still can?"

Brigitte looked up. What was that supposed to mean?

He brushed a stray hair out of his eye. "You know you're going to lose," he continued listlessly. "You'll save yourself a lot of pain if you quit now instead of running yourself ragged trying to beat me."

Wh-what did he just say...?

The muscles in her face twitched as he stared blankly down at her. Whether he noticed, he continued his verbal attack. "I hate to say this, but studying for a couple of weeks isn't going to do it. You know that, don't you?"

"...!"

His tone aside, she had to admit the point. But she still didn't want to nod meekly and agree. Otherwise...she would be rejecting the whole being of the shivering little girl in her dream.

I don't want to lose!

That was her sole emotion.

Brigitte jumped to her feet and pointed at Yuri's chest.

"Neither of us knows how this will end. You're so full of yourself now, but that means you will be even more embarrassed when I beat you!" she shouted, her shrill voice echoing through the library.

Yuri's eyes widened very slightly in surprise. But a second later, the expression was gone.

"...That so?"

"Yes, it is!"

"Your attitude's impressive, if nothing else."

"My test scores will be far more impressive than my attitude, so you'd better be ready!"

"Um, excuse me, but would you mind keeping your voices down...?"

Once again, they were being scolded by the librarian in glasses, whose head was poking timidly through the door.

"...I'm sorry," Brigitte said, blushing as she covered her mouth.

I lost my temper again...

This was a library. Silence was sacred. No one was in the study area, but the stacks were another story. Maybe a student had complained to the librarian. Maybe she would even be banned from the library for being too loud. That would be a problem. There were so many books she still wanted to read.

I'd better be more careful...

As she stood there turning various colors, Yuri sighed.

"Well, I'm leaving. My ears are ringing, probably because of that squawking bird I just heard."

"...I'm so sorry to hear that. Please take care of yourself," Brigitte said, pretending not to catch his sarcasm.

But Yuri must have sensed her glaring at his retreating form because he turned back after opening the door.

"...What?" she said.

"...You too."

"Excuse me?"

"If you're not feeling well, you should see a doctor."

With that, he strode off. She stood staring at the door for a while, then mulled over his words.

Was he implying her voice was so grating, she should see a doctor?

Or maybe...

...Is he genuinely worried about me?

Was he saying she should get some rest because she seemed unwell?

…As soon as the thought struck her, she shook her head. *Ridiculous.*

She couldn't let the enemy see any more of her weaknesses. She began packing up her open notebooks—maybe she wouldn't push herself quite so hard.

CHAPTER 3

Tempestuous Tests

The big day is finally here...!

On the morning of the tests, Brigitte rose an hour earlier than usual, completed her routine, and left the house. The carriage ride was too rocky for her to study...but as she gazed out the window, she was mentally reviewing the subjects she was weakest in.

The written tests were scheduled to take the whole day. The subjects were human sciences, history, fundamentals of magic, applied magic, spiritology, and medicinal herbology. During midterms, these exams were followed by practical tests the next day, but this time, she thankfully didn't need to worry about that.

When she arrived in her classroom, she sat down, took out her notebook, and started reviewing for the last time.

Magic is easy because most of it has to do with spirits. And medicinal plants aren't bad, either, because most of them are the favorite of some spirit.

She was very good at history, too, as spirits were integral to the kingdom's story. Her main interest made studying the subject quite easy.

But this time, she was up against Yuri Aurealis, the supposed genius. If she intended to emerge victorious, she couldn't make a single mistake.

...But I'm going to win! I'm going to win and make him pay!

Fiercely determined, she flipped through her notes on human studies, the first subject on the test.

By midday, the first three exams were over. Feeling good about her performance, Brigitte ate lunch in the cafeteria and then returned to the classroom.

Before Joseph had broken off their engagement, she used to eat with him in one of the five semiprivate cafeteria booths. Enclosed by elegant wine-red curtains, the spacious booths were a favorite of the students with the highest status and for that reason were nicknamed the "salons." Using them was a way of showing off their family standing and power.

They were a special place for Brigitte—but not for Joseph, apparently. These days, she could hear him laughing and talking with Lisa in there.

...Right. Next up, applied magic.

She exhaled softly to push away the thoughts of Joseph.

The applied magic and spiritology tests went well. During the break after spiritology, she walked to the restroom near her class. The only test left was medicinal herbology, but since it was one of her strong subjects, she felt confident. When she got back to the classroom, she dug through her bag to find what she needed for the test...and discovered something.

Puzzled, she looked through her bag again. But it wasn't there.

...I can't believe this.

She was stunned.

My pen case is gone.

She had carefully put her pen case away after the last test, but it was gone without a trace. She checked around her desk and near the window just to be sure, but it wasn't there, either.

Someone must have stolen it.

Frowning, she bit her lip. She didn't know who'd done it, but the theft itself seemed certain. After all, even the extra pens she'd brought were gone.

She'd never before been the victim of such crude harassment. She knew there were plenty of rumors circulating about her. But she had been the prince's fiancée, so no one had dared make such an overt move against her before. Maybe she'd benefited from Joseph's presence more than she realized—although she was hardly in a mood to feel grateful for it.

...I suppose I can buy one...

There was a little shop next to the cafeteria, although she'd never bought anything there. But it took only a few seconds for her to realize that it was closed today for the tests. Everything was against her. And it was a rule that on test days, students had to bring everything they needed themselves. Asking a teacher would result in an automatic score of zero.

"What do I do...?" she couldn't help muttering as her panic ballooned. She wasn't close enough with any of her classmates to ask to borrow a pen. No wind spirit was going to float one over to her, and no earth spirit was going to find one for her dropped in a gutter.

For a brief second, she thought of her adopted brother, a class below her—or more accurately, she thought of his hazy back. But she quickly shook her head, banishing those fantasies.

If my father heard about that, he'd be furious...

She didn't put it past him to spy on her at school to make sure she didn't talk to her brother. If she did, their father might punish both of them, too. Dragging him into this was the last thing she wanted to do. And even if she did ask him, she was doubtful an adopted brother she'd hardly even met would lend her a pen.

Let's see, who else...? I can't think of anyone.

She was at her wits' end. She knew it was her fault. She knew the reason she didn't have any friends was her own arrogant, unpleasant attitude. But just for today, she had wanted to focus entirely on the test.

This was supposed to be about my competition with Yuri...

She thought of his dispassionate eyes. To make matters worse, he was a genius. If she got a zero in one subject, everything was over. That was how smart he was, and that was why she wanted so badly to beat him. She imagined having to admit she'd stupidly lost her pens after boasting with such confidence before.

She could just see him muttering, *That so?* as his beautiful eyes turned dull. He would lose interest when he learned she had nothing better to offer and that all she could do was make a stupid excuse for losing. Then he'd forget all about the silly redhead.

No matter what, I want to beat him!

She had an idea. This was no time to split hairs over the means to her end. Her mind was made up: Even if she fought dirty, she had to fight.

"Please take your seats. The next test will now begin."

The medicinal herbology teacher walked into the classroom.

"..."

Brigitte gulped and grasped the object she needed between her pointer finger and thumb.

Three days had passed since the tests.

That was exhausting...

Finally released from her scolding, Brigitte walked out of the teachers' office. Stretching her tense muscles, she stopped by the bulletin board on the first floor. She'd seen the test results at lunch, but she wanted to check one more time.

Suddenly, she felt someone watching her and turned around. Several students quickly averted their eyes.

It feels like people are staring more than usual today...

But she didn't have time to think past that. She was already late for her meeting with Yuri. Worried that he might have left, she ran down the stone path. To her relief, she saw his distinctive blue-black hair in the distance. A thick applied magic textbook was lying on the table. He must have been reviewing the test while he waited for her.

"I'm sorry to make you wait," she said, catching her breath.

"I wasn't waiting," he answered, sprawled arrogantly in his chair.

Is he incapable of letting a single sentence go by without commentary? Will he not be able to sleep otherwise?

Realizing the same could be said of her, she sat down across from the blank-faced Yuri. There was something she had to say.

"Congratulations on taking first place, Yuri Aurealis."

"...Yeah," he said flatly, dipping his head slightly.

In the year and two months since he started at the academy, he had gotten close to a perfect score on every test. Each of the six subjects was worth one hundred points, and this time he had achieved an illustrious 598.

"And you?"

"..."

"What was your score?"

"..."

She turned away. He looked at her suspiciously. Her impulse was to say nothing, but this was a historic battle. Silence would not do.

"...four hundred and ninety-eight," she muttered. She'd double-checked.

"Huh. Exactly one hundred less than me."

Ouch!

She had no response to the merciless truth. True, her score was far better than in the past. But compared to the top students on the bulletin board, with Yuri above them all, it was nothing.

"That's true...unfortunately."

It's not unfortunate at all...

It was actually so frustrating, she wanted to scream. She'd meant to win. She'd longed to beat this detestable boy hollow.

But I couldn't.

"I lost the competition," she said meekly.

"Why don't you say why?" Yuri asked out of nowhere.

She was confused. "What do you mean?"

"...You wrote your answers to the medicinal herbology test in blood, didn't you?"

"!"

She stared at him. He didn't seem the type to care about gossip, so how did he know that? Had the rumors spread even further than she realized?

"The teacher told us about it in class today. He was furious."

That teacher...

He had the nerve to tell other classes about it?! Maybe that was why everyone had been staring at her when she stopped by the bulletin board earlier.

If Yuri knew, she'd be hard-pressed to avoid telling him the rest. Covering her mouth with her fan, she haltingly began explaining the whole story.

"Well, I...I did do that. Because someone stole my pens."

"Your pens were stolen?"

"I don't know who. Plenty of people hate me now."

She'd gotten through the test with sheer perseverance—so of course she had been upset when the teacher thrust her answer sheet back with a zero written on it so big, she couldn't argue. Before meeting with Yuri, the teacher had called her to the office and lectured her incessantly about it. His face had been beet red as he pounded her answer sheet on his desk and ranted about making a fool of her teachers with her undignified behavior.

Maybe I did have another option.

Maybe it would have been more sensible to give up on the whole subject test.

But Brigitte didn't regret her actions. If anything, she was proud of her decision to use the pin on her uniform brooch to prick her fingertip and mark the answers in blood. Her right pointer finger was still bandaged, but that was hidden by her gloves. No one would notice except Sienna, who had seen right through her and given her a good scolding.

"Why didn't you ask to borrow mine?" Yuri asked.

She was so lost in thought, it took her a few seconds to respond.

...What did he say? She must have misheard him.

But he just pressed his lips together sullenly and said nothing.

"If I asked...would you have lent one to me?" she asked timidly.

"Well...," he said, apparently caught off guard. He rested his chin in his hand...and after a few moments, reluctantly mumbled, "...I suppose it wouldn't have been out of the question."

"...So you would have considered it?"

He had a very indirect way of phrasing his thoughts, but she guessed that must be what he meant. The thought made her feel just a tiny bit better.

Maybe that's strange given the kind of person I'm dealing with here.

If she ever ran into more unexpected trouble...she wondered if she would feel less like a lost child with no one to turn to.

"Then if something like this happens again, I'll count on you," she said.

"...If something like this happens again, shouldn't you try to figure out who did it?"

"That sounds like so much trouble for nothing...considering I'm the most hated person in this school."

Yuri looked slightly amused that she was boasting about having so many enemies. She had never seen the remotest hint of vulnerability from him before, and she blinked in surprise...but a moment later, his icy expression was back. On second thought, maybe it was all in her head.

"I think I can rival you on that count."

"I—I suppose you can."

She was going to contradict him, but then she realized he was right and nodded solemnly instead. Immediately, he looked so affronted that Brigitte couldn't help laughing. She pressed her palms to her cheeks and sighed.

"Mr. Aurealis, you remind me of a storybook villain."

"You're a fine one to talk... Or were you trying to be sympathetic? Spare me the hassle."

"What?!"

If I say black, he just says white!

She'd lost her cool again, but he didn't bat an eyelash. Far from it—he was staring at her earnestly. Her heart skipped a beat.

"Does your finger hurt?" he asked, his gaze falling to her gloved hands. He seemed to be worried about her.

"...It's f-fine. Just a little scratch."

"That so? ...Next time, don't do that, all right?"

His voice sounded so kind she couldn't manage an answer. In

the end, she just nodded silently, and he backed off. But only as far as her finger was concerned.

"And? When you added up your points, what was your score on the medicinal herbology test?"

"I..."

She hesitated, but he stared pointedly at her. He didn't look ready to let her go home without telling him. Resigning herself, she decided to admit the truth.

"I got a perfect score...which makes 598 points total."

"I see."

He nodded, apparently unsurprised. Neither did he seem to doubt her. But she still felt incredibly awkward.

I didn't want to tell him that...

It was hard to explain—but it made her sound like a poor loser. It was like saying that the only reason she hadn't joined him at first place was because someone took her pens.

The point is, my actual score was 498! That hasn't changed!

She frowned, but his next words weren't what she expected.

"You're good at studying, aren't you?"

"Um..."

"If you can get a score like that with a couple of weeks of shallow effort, you must have a gift."

The unspoken implication was *And you don't, do you?*

Brigitte pouted behind her fan. As much as she hated to admit it, he was right. She wasn't a genius, and she wasn't unusually good at memorization. It was simply that she'd been reading academic books since she was little, so she had plenty of facts in her head. The past few weeks were just review.

"Is there another reason?" he asked.

She hesitated, but ultimately, she didn't know what else to do and picked up the thick text on the table. She could tell as she flipped through it that it was well used. Yuri didn't seem angry, but he didn't take his intense gaze off her. If she told him, would he make fun of her? She knew the answer right away.

He won't laugh.

He was extremely rude, but she guessed that he wouldn't laugh at someone's dreams without good reason.

"...I want to study spirits," she said stiffly.

"Be a spiritologist, you mean?" he asked bluntly. That was exactly what she'd been trying to avoid saying.

She coughed. "Yes, a spiritologist... It's been my dream since I was a little girl."

"Mommy, Daddy, I wanna know more about spiwits."

She had said that to her family—until the day of the contracting ceremony. Her father and mother had always told her that she was a smart little girl. Back then, they had called her a child prodigy.

In truth, they must have thought her dream was ridiculous. But they had let her have it, as a child's fantasy. Her father had said he was sure that a wonderful spirit would take a fancy to her and give her its protection. And she had believed unquestioningly in that bright future. She had imagined herself traveling the world as a spiritologist alongside her faithful companion.

"...I'm contracted with a tiny spirit...but I've never felt sad about that."

"...Why not?"

"A spirit's a spirit. Mine hasn't shown itself to me yet, but I call to it every day."

Brigitte still didn't know the name of the spirit that had given her its protection or what it looked like. But she was happy, because it had chosen her and no one else. No matter what other people said, she would never turn against her spirit.

"...They say most spiritologists have disappeared, you know."

Of course it was like him to know such a thing, even worry about it.

Brigitte looked down and nodded.

"...I know. They say the spirits come to like them too much and drag them into the spirit world."

One of the spiritologists Brigitte respected—Lien Baluanuki, the author of *The Wind Laughs*—had vanished from the public eye some twenty years earlier. Since he was elderly, people speculated he had died while studying spirits in some desolate place...but a more plausible rumor was that the sylphide had led him into the spirit world.

Brigitte laughed. "If ever I have the chance, I'd like to go to the spirit world myself one day!"

Yuri stared silently at her. People who crossed to the spirit world could never return to the earthly one. That was the generally accepted theory. Maybe Yuri took her words as a death wish—but as she expected, he said nothing.

...I was right; he's not laughing at me.

Brigitte was glad. After so many years of mockery, it was secretly reassuring to be with someone who didn't laugh like everyone else. Maybe that was why, for once, she had no trouble expressing her gratitude.

"Thank you for listening, Mr. Aurealis."

"I didn't do anything special."

"You did it the other day, too—you listened to what I had to say."

We were here in the gazebo that day...and I told him all sorts of things without being embarrassed, even though we'd just met.

She wondered why. A man everyone called the Frozen Blade and avoided wasn't exactly an ideal conversation partner for personal topics. But even though his rudeness put her off, she kept sharing more and more about herself. About the things she'd locked away in her heart because no one would listen—about her past.

I wonder if he'll ever tell me about himself.

She gazed at him, briefly hopeful, then stopped herself. Their competition was over, and he'd won. She'd probably have nothing more to do with him. The thought...created a brief pang in her chest.

"Guess we'll have to wait till next time for a rematch."

"Huh?"

"This time was a draw. You got the same score I did."

The same score?

Brigitte didn't know what to say.

"But, Mr. Aurealis—"

"Call me Yuri," he interrupted curtly. "I don't like to be called by my family name."

"...Sir Yuri, then?"

He nodded his consent, and Brigitte's eyes sparkled. She'd been looking for her chance to say something, and this seemed to be it.

"In that case, please call me Brigitte instead of 'you.'"

"...You—"

"*Brigitte,*" she said more firmly.

He was momentarily silent. Her gaze remained bright and strong, and eventually, he seemed to give up on resisting.

"Fine. Brigitte."

"!"

"Are you satisfied?"

Although he looked supremely annoyed, she grinned and nodded.

"I am, Sir Yuri!"

After all, this seemed to mean he intended to keep talking to her. It was a little thing, but it made her unbearably happy.

Behind the wine-red curtains, Lisa was holding an elegant after-school tea party with her closest girlfriends. Recently, one of her favorite pastimes was having tea with all the fanciest accoutrements.

She knew that there had historically been a tacit understanding at Otoleanna Academy that the five luxurious semiprivate rooms in the cafeteria were to be used only by high nobles—but since they were seldom occupied, she had taken the liberty of occupying one.

After all, Lisa was going to be engaged to Joseph, a prince. No one would blame her for using the room, and she was entitled to it as a noble.

…But this tea party was supposed to be pleasant, and unwanted noise kept seeping in from the outside world to spoil Lisa's fun.

"Hey, did you hear about Brigitte Meidell's test scores?"

"Of course I did! I could hardly believe it!"

"Aren't you in the same class as the Red Fairy?"

Lisa drummed the table with her pointy nails. Once again, those idiots were making a racket over stupid rumors.

Damn, it's driving me mad…

"Do you think we were wrong all along? What if the Red Fairy's not so useless after a—"

"Shut up!!" she finally shrieked, pounding the table with all her might. The teacups jumped, sloshing black tea over the table.

The world beyond the curtain went silent.

A moment later, she heard footsteps hurrying away...but her mood did not improve.

"Miss Lisa..."

The dithering anxiety of her clique only made her angrier. She glared at them, and they all flinched.

"...Don't you think it's odd?"

"What is?"

"Why, that Brigitte of all people ranked thirtieth in our grade!!"

Lisa ground her teeth together. This was stupid, brainless Brigitte Meidell they were talking about. The haughty Red Fairy had been tossed aside by Joseph the Third Prince about a month ago. She had awful grades and was famous for always scoring near the bottom on written tests. Lately, she'd been spotted studying non-stop, as if she'd lost her mind after the broken engagement—and Lisa had jeered at her behind her back.

She'd also decided to interfere with her chances on the written exam.

Of course, Brigitte would probably fail even without Lisa's help. Lisa knew that, but just to be safe, she had ordered a student in Brigitte's class to steal her pens.

"...You did steal her pens, didn't you?!" Lisa demanded harshly.

"...Y-yes," the cowardly girl answered in a voice quieter than a breath.

Lisa didn't know how many times she'd asked that question.

The girl was sitting in the corner shivering, her long, pitch-black bangs hiding her face. Lisa was about to interrogate her some more...but changed her mind at the last minute.

After all, she knew full well Brigitte had run into trouble. It took less than a day for the unbelievably ridiculous story about her writing her answers to the medicinal herbology test in blood to get around. Lisa had taken advantage of that. She'd stirred up the rumors by commenting loudly wherever she went about how barbaric it was to take a test in blood, and how the Red Fairy had literally covered herself in red, and how she was obviously heartbroken over losing the love of her kind prince.

But Lisa still couldn't help grinding her teeth.

What...? How...?

As it turned out, Brigitte somehow managed to place thirtieth out of a hundred students.

But I was...eighty-seventh!

Even more shockingly, Brigitte had been given a score of zero on the medicinal herbology test. And since the teacher had grumbled about it, every second-year student knew the truth by now—that if she'd written in pen, she would have aced the test.

In other words...

If Lisa hadn't made that girl steal her pens, Brigitte's name would have been up there in a tie with the perpetual number-one student, Yuri.

There's no way! No damn way!

As Lisa watched helplessly, the news spread like wildfire through the school. No doubt the outraged teacher had intended to make an example of her. But thanks to him, the whole school now knew that she should have scored first, not thirtieth. The fuss was more than enough to overshadow the writing-in-blood incident.

"I just don't get it...! Someone like her can't possibly be smart!" Lisa screamed, mussing her carefully set curls. "This is Brigitte Meidell, the biggest idiot in school! She must have cheated! Don't you think so?!"

"Miss Lisa..."

The other girls exchanged looks as if to say, *How in the world do we answer that question?* This infuriated Lisa even more.

What's wrong with these people...? Why don't they agree with me...?!

Just then, she heard a low voice.

"...Interesting."

"...?!"

It was clearly coming from the other side of the divider. Lisa jumped up noisily, pushed her girlfriends aside, and stepped out of the booth.

She narrowed her eyes. The curtain of the neighboring booth was pulled shut.

I don't know who's in there, but they're eavesdropping!

Without pausing to think, she yanked open the curtain.

She had completely forgotten that private rooms were intended for high nobles who far outranked her.

"How dare you—," she began, but as soon as she saw who was inside, she gasped.

A boy with blue-black hair was sitting alone in the room.

Lisa was in shock.

"Sir Y-Yuri..."

It was Yuri Aurealis.

Not only was he rumored to be a genius even within the illustrious Water Clan, he was so handsome that many found it difficult to talk to him.

Lisa could hear her girlfriends, who had followed her, shifting around wordlessly. Plenty of girls wanted to date him, but his cold treatment of them had earned him the name the Frozen Blade. Just days before, Lisa herself had gotten a shock when Yuri gave her the same treatment, and she'd complained to Joseph about it. But when Joseph confronted him, he hadn't blinked. Instead, he had eyed her with profound disinterest.

"Wh-what are you doing here, Sir Yuri...?"

"Just a coincidence," he answered without looking at her. An empty saucer and teacup were on the table before him.

After wiping his mouth delicately with a napkin, he finally turned in her direction. As soon as his eyes fell on her, a chill ran down her back. His gaze truly was icy and sharp as a knife.

"...Anyhow, I never expected that the thieves who took Brigitte's pens would be having a *private chat* in a place like this."

Every one of them gaped.

He'd heard them. He'd heard everything they said.

But that wasn't the part that bothered Lisa.

He just called her Brigitte...

Why would Yuri use her first name, as if they were friends? Lisa couldn't figure it out. After all, the handsome duke's son brushed away the most beautiful girls like they were flies.

"I...I'm sorry, I..."

Before Lisa had time to think, the girl who had stolen the pen case was bowing apologetically to him.

"There's no point in apologizing to me," he snapped back. "How about apologizing to Brigitte?"

"To Miss Meidell...?"

"Don't worry. Her bark's worse than her bite."

"..."

The black-haired girl bowed to Yuri again, then left the cafeteria. Lisa was angry that the girl had left without saying good-bye, but she didn't have time to worry about trifles like that right now. Desperately trying to calm her emotions, Lisa glared at Yuri insolently.

"Do you plan to t-tell anyone about this?"

"...?"

Yuri looked suspiciously at her.

"Be warned—if I tell His Highness Joseph, it will be the end for you! You'll be tossed right out of this school! It'd serve you right, too!" she said.

"But if I tell a teacher what you did first, won't you be the one whose future is in jeopardy?"

"...!"

Lisa was dumbfounded. Yuri gazed at her with boredom.

"...Brigitte and I were competing for the top score on that test."

"What...?"

Why in the world would Sir Yuri compete with someone like Brigitte?

The whole world had turned upside down. But Yuri just sighed and pierced her with his merciless, icy gaze, and she forgot to breathe.

"...I was having a serious competition, and I don't appreciate the interference. Let me just say that if you do this again, I will not stand idly by."

"...?!"

Pure terror was crawling down Lisa's spine. Overwhelmed, she took a few steps back...until she tripped over her own feet and ended up on her rear end. The loud crash made her feel even more foolish.

Yuri just glanced at her, unsmiling, and strode off with his uniform billowing behind him.

"M-Miss Lisa...!"

"Are you all right, Miss Lisa...?"

As Lisa sat frozen on the ground, her clique tried to help her stand up. But it was several minutes of calling her name before she was able to answer.

CHAPTER 4

Brigitte's Slumbering Power

"You seem very happy lately," Sienna said abruptly as Brigitte was sipping a cup of black tea.

Brigitte stopped turning the page of the book she was reading and jerked her head up. She had been enjoying some quiet reading time on the balcony of her cottage. She loved this little space off her room with a view of the garden. She could survey the garden that Hans tended each day…and since it was on the opposite side of the cottage from the main residence, she didn't have to worry about her parents seeing her.

I'll bet that was why they built it on this side.

Unable to regain her composure, she stared at Sienna.

"…I do?" she asked timidly.

Sienna nodded, her face blank. "Yes. Very happy."

Very?!

She couldn't imagine that. For some reason, when she tried to think of an explanation, a certain person came to mind.

Yuri Aurealis…

The day before, he had snorted at her hesitation to check out a book for the first time.

"While you were wasting time worrying about that, I finished this whole book," he said...

Infuriated by his provocative attitude, she'd practically run to the counter and checked out the book. The librarian with the glasses had startled at Brigitte's intensity, but she checked out the book without a hitch.

In other words, Yuri had given her the shove she needed—and she was poring over that very book right now.

"Is it because you did so well on the exams?"

"That?! Oh...yes, I suppose. You might be right," Brigitte answered, flustered.

Sienna gave her a hard look. "...I want you to promise that you will never ever prick your finger to take a test again."

"I, er, don't have any plans to. Don't worry."

Sienna had extracted the same promise that morning as she changed the bandage on Brigitte's finger. Brigitte knew it was behavior unbefitting a lady...but she was surprised both by the ferocity of Sienna's anger and the reason for it.

"At the very least, use my blood next time. That would be much better than hurting yourself."

When she saw the mixture of anger and concern on Sienna's normally expressionless face, she felt awful. She hadn't yet told Sienna that she'd been competing for first place on that test with the son of the Water Clan—whom she now knew well enough to call an acquaintance.

The only places Brigitte talked with Yuri were the library and the gazebo. Maybe that was why she still felt a certain distance... if that was the word for it.

But I don't feel lonely because of it—or sorry.

She made up excuses to herself, not understanding her own feelings.

Meanwhile, Sienna was clearly puzzled. "…Miss Brigitte? Is something wrong?"

"N-no—nothing. I'm fine." She coughed. "Sienna, I'd like to concentrate on this book."

"Yes, miss. Please call me if you need anything."

Sienna softly retreated. There was nothing unusual in Brigitte's request, and Sienna didn't appear to be suspicious. Brigitte picked up her cup and pretended to drink some tea as she glanced around her room.

Sienna was gone. She was probably in the hallway already.

Once she was sure of this, Brigitte set her cup silently on the saucer. She stood from her chair, squatted, and peered through the bars of the balcony to scan the grounds.

Right, the garden is empty…

She didn't see Hans or any other servant returning from an errand. For once, Carson, the assistant cook and pâtissier, wasn't scurrying around the garden. Brigitte nodded to herself, leaned against the banister, and took a deep breath.

"Hey…spirit!" she whispered very quietly.

She was looking up at empty air. She had no other choice, since she had no idea where the spirit she was calling might be or what it might be doing.

"If you can hear me, I would love for you to answer. Or perhaps you could show yourself for a moment?"

There was no answer.

Brigitte wasn't disappointed, since this was what always happened. She took a stone from a hiding spot and held it above her head.

"This is a magic fire stone. Please accept it as a token of friendship."

Magic stones were often used to communicate with spirits.

Although they glittered like jewels, there was a crucial difference—they held the source of magical power.

Spirits had souls. They lent many powers to people they had a special fondness for, and if such a person was in danger, they sometimes materialized to offer aid. It had long been standard practice to please the spirit you were contracted with by offering presents associated with their type.

Brigitte had been talking to her spirit nearly every day since she was five years old, and every weekend she offered a present like this one. She had tried countless presents with no luck. Today she was going back to the basics with a magic fire stone.

I do think even tiny spirits must have souls...

That was her personal theory. So far, there were no records of communication with tiny spirits—what people called no-names. But even people who contracted with tiny spirits were able to perform low-level "daily-life magic." Brigitte saw this as evidence that they did have souls and that they lent their power to those they contracted with.

Although I can't even do daily-life magic...

"...I just want to meet you!" she shouted childishly.

The more she thought about it, the more worked up she got.

"I want to meet you and talk, even just once! I want to ask you about yourself and about the land you live in! And if you don't m-mind—I would love to borrow just a tiny bit of your power..."

Just then, she sensed someone behind her and spun around.

Sienna was standing there, expressionless. Or, to be more accurate, she was smiling very slightly.

Brigitte froze.

Sienna bowed gracefully. "I'm very sorry. I called your name several times."

"...!"

"Miss Brigitte, Carson has made a grape tart that he would like you to try..."

"Sienna, you're laughing at me, aren't you?!"

Sienna was momentarily silent. Then she shook her head. "No... I'm not laughing, but I just couldn't help smiling a little at how sweet you are..."

"You're laughing!"

Possibly to keep herself from laughing at her blushing mistress, Sienna puffed up one cheek, and Brigitte realized that Sienna was shaking.

Brigitte writhed in shame.

"I'm sorry, miss. It's just that I've never heard anyone call their spirit by saying '*Hey*,' before."

"You were listening to all of it?!"

"Anyway, what about the grape tart?"

"I'd like some!!"

Still in a huff, she walked back into her room from the balcony, and Sienna followed. Sienna knew very well that her adorable mistress would cheer right up once she ate something sweet...so she didn't feel very sorry.

That was why neither of them noticed when the magic fire stone left behind on the table floated into the air—and vanished without a trace.

"Our next class will be about building a relationship with a spirit. Your practical assignment will be to demonstrate your communication with the spirit you are contracted with."

The following day, as Brigitte listened to her spiritology teacher explain their assignment, she felt like she was receiving a death sentence—even though she normally adored spiritology.

She had been told when she began at the academy that starting in the second year, there would be a greater emphasis on practical skills. Her fellow students loved to talk about what tricks would get the highest grades.

And I haven't even met my spirit yet...

She was tempted to wonder if this was some sort of punishment for taking her test with her blood, but she knew her spiritology teacher, Marjory Naha, would never do something like that.

Marjory Naha was a gentle, pretty, elderly lady, so kind that when she heard about Brigitte's test in blood, she asked worriedly if her injury had been properly treated. Brigitte trusted Ms. Naha because she was always fair, unlike the other teachers.

From now on, as Ms. Naha said, class would focus on more practical aspects of communication with spirits and use of their magic.

I lost that magic stone, too...

Brigitte sighed softly in her seat by the window. The day before, she had deliberately asked Sienna to buy a nice stone to give her spirit, not from one of those shabby stalls, but from a real stone shop.

As an outcast in her own family, Brigitte had almost no money to spend as she wished, so she had to rely on the allowance she had saved up since childhood. The butler was given a monthly sum for her clothing and makeup, but even she wasn't bold enough to ask him to use it to pay for magic stones.

I've seen students working at the library after school...

But she probably wouldn't be allowed to do that. Even though she wasn't accepted as a member of the family, she was forbidden from doing anything that would bring shame to the Meidell name.

Thinking about all of that was starting to leave a bad taste in her mouth, even when it came to her beloved spiritology.

She stood up and noticed a fellow student in front of her.

"Miss Meidell."

She frowned.

It's Nival Weir...

His face was handsome but stern, and he did not smile as he said her name. As the second son of Viscount Weir, he was viewed as a candidate for Joseph's assistant in the future. He was also an outstanding student and had been class president since their first year.

Brigitte didn't have a very good impression of him, however, since he'd always seemed to sneer at her when she was with Joseph.

Because students at Otoleanna Academy stayed in the same class group for all three years, she had spent the past year and several months in the same room with him, and his antipathy toward her was only growing more obvious.

He probably thought I wasn't fit to be the prince's fiancée. I can understand why!

"Congratulations on your test score," he said.

"...I'm not sure my standing was high enough to deserve congratulations."

For a second, he stared at her—then smiled.

"...Everyone is so surprised. After all, your grades have always been poor," he went on. "Did your spirit help you out?"

Now I see what he's after.

She narrowed her eyes. This explained why he'd sought her out despite his clear dislike for her. The teacher had been so furious about her answering in blood that he had turned her perfect score into a zero. Nival knew that, of course. He was openly accusing her of having cheated to achieve the top score she would have had if not for that teacher. Because, of course, the Red Fairy could never achieve something like that on her own.

This is so annoying...

She wanted to walk off without a word, but that would be like admitting she'd cheated. Instead, she answered loud enough for all the students listening in to hear.

"As you know, I am contracted with a tiny spirit...so I am not able to get that sort of help on my tests."

"True. Your spirit is so weak it's useless for even the most basic tasks... Oh, excuse me."

He placed his hand over his mouth, as if he'd said that by accident.

Brigitte was sick of it.

A quiet anger rose in her.

Just because her nameless spirit had contracted with her, it had to suffer being called a fool. So typical. This had been her life for the past ten-some years. But she had resolved to be positive. She wouldn't laugh it off and cry later, like she used to.

If people want to fight with me, I ought to fight back.

"That reminds me, you're contracted with a wind spirit, aren't you?"

Nival must have sensed that she was acting differently than usual; his face twisted uncomfortably.

"...What about it?"

"I just remembered there was an incident here at school a few years back involving wind magic."

He looked sullenly at her as she tilted her head, as if to say, *You haven't heard?* He didn't seem to know to what she was referring. All the better. She moved her hands lightly in front of her chest as she explained.

"A certain student used wind magic to raise and tilt the

answer sheet of a smart student very slightly so they could read the answers."

She shook her head to suggest how regrettable it was.

"Imagine wasting your magical gifts on something so trivial as that...don't you agree?"

"...I suppose."

"And wasn't it just yesterday that I saw you suddenly opening the classroom windows before our fundamentals of magic test? Could that have been...?"

"...?! I'm no cheater!" he cried, and even Brigitte recoiled at the volume. She covered her mouth in surprise—but by this time, all eyes were on Nival, not her. Brigitte smiled, pretending not to notice.

"But I never implied you were! I simply wanted to thank you for freshening up the air in the classroom."

"...!!"

He glared at her, but she didn't bat an eyelash. In the past, she probably wouldn't have been able to take such a strong stand against him. The difference now was that...

Next to Yuri's eyes, his are like a pleasant breeze...

He was a sweet young thing compared to the boy they called the Frozen Blade. She couldn't help smiling.

"Was there anything else?" she asked Nival.

"...No..."

Perhaps noticing that his luck had changed, Nival muttered something about being busy and hurried off. With all eyes back on her, Brigitte packed up her books and left the classroom.

I doubt Yuri would ever say something so vulgar to me, she thought as she walked down the hallway.

As she imagined his face, her pounding heart gradually calmed.

He's incredibly sarcastic, but he would never question someone's ability or find fault with their work...

Just then, Brigitte realized something.

Why am I thinking about him all the time?!

She shook her head vigorously, trying to wipe away the fresh image of his face that rose in her mind. Forget about him—she needed to concentrate on her spiritology assignment. The next class was two days from now. Before then, she had to come up with a strategy for engaging her tiny spirit. And who knew more about spirits than—?

Yes! I'd like to ask Yuri his advice!

As she hurried toward the library, she didn't even realize that she was thinking about him again.

Since she couldn't find him anywhere in the library, she walked to the gazebo. She was certain she'd find him there, but he was not in his usual chair. Heaving a deep sigh, she looked around.

"...I wonder if he's not coming today," she mumbled.

She and Yuri weren't friends or anything close to it. They had no standing arrangement to meet every day. There was nothing strange in the fact that he wasn't there.

Yet I'm so disappointed...

Disappointed with herself, she was about to leave when she heard an unfamiliar noise. She turned around.

I hear water. Maybe...

She ran down the stone stairs next to the gazebo, toward the distinct burbling.

A stream ran below the garden next to the library, with a large forest beyond it. Sometimes students went into the forest for extracurricular classes, but she'd never entered from the library side. She was breathing fast from excitement at the novelty of it—but that wasn't the only reason.

There he is!

At the bottom of the stairs, a dry twig snapped under her foot.

Yuri, who had his back to her, turned sharply. She thought she saw the stern caution in his eyes soften very slightly when he realized it was her.

"...Oh, it's you."

"Sir Yuri."

She sighed in relief. A second later, she saw a spirit hovering in the water directly in front of him.

An undine!

Before thinking, Brigitte blurted out, "She's so beautiful...!"

"My, what an innocent young lady."

Brigitte flushed as the smiling undine answered her.

When it came to first-class water spirits, undines were always the first that came to mind. Floating in midair, her feet seeming to melt into the brook, this one waved her webbed hand in apparent greeting. Spirits were said to lack personalities in the human sense, but with her feminine, fluid form, she was breathtaking. Her voice, which seemed to echo faintly from a distance, was so pleasing that Brigitte wanted to listen to it forever.

Her face is so refined and flawless and well-shaped...

How gorgeous she was. Brigitte stared, completely captivated, until Yuri pulled her back to reality with a "hey!"

She bowed her head, flustered. "I've n-never had the pleasure of speaking with a first-class spirit before... Please forgive me for getting overly excited!"

I can see why so many men end up as their prisoners...!

Yuri let out an exasperated sigh. Brigitte shrank back slightly, embarrassed to have been captured so easily by the charm of the spirit, especially since he knew about her dream.

"You've never spoken to one? But the Earl of Meidell must have several of them."

"He does...and I've seen them, but he doesn't allow me to speak to them."

"...Is that so?" Yuri glanced away.

Am I wrong, or is the mood suddenly heavy?

"Wh-what about your other spirit?" she asked, changing the subject.

"My what?"

"Aren't you contracted with two first-class spirits?"

Typically, spirits—especially first-class spirits like undines—did not show themselves in the human world spontaneously. The spirit Brigitte was looking at had to be one that Yuri was contracted with. She had assumed the other one must be nearby.

"Oh, that one..." He hesitated, which was unlike him. "...That one's not feeling well and won't come out right now."

"Oh, I see..."

Of course, she didn't want him to force the spirit to manifest.

"My, my," the undine said, resting a hand on her cheek. She leaned toward Brigitte, her beautiful body glittering as if the sunlight were embracing it. "Look at that fiery red hair. Are you by chance a daughter of the Fire Clan?"

"Yes, I am. My name is Brigitte Meidell," she said, her heart pounding.

The undine laughed knowingly. "Then you're contracted with an ifrit?"

"...No. I...I'm contracted with a tiny spirit."

"Are you, now?" the undine said, resting a finger on her chin—or the equivalent of it. "...My master is called the Frozen Blade. What are you called?"

"...The Red Fairy," she answered hesitantly.

The undine nodded merrily. "The Red Fairy. What a lovely name."

"...Is it?" Brigitte smiled wryly. She knew the term was a euphemism for a changeling, a nasty rumor she refused to accept.

"Oh yes. It's a perfect name for you, Brigitte."

Brigitte felt like she'd been poked in the heart with a tiny needle.

"This is not my child!"

Eleven years earlier, feverish from her wounds that wouldn't heal, she had heard her father's angry voice, far away, repeating those words again and again. Her mother's voice, crying hysterically. Her father, hurling abuse at her.

"My true child was carried away to the spirit world, with a changeling left in her place!"

If so, then the Red Fairy would be a fitting name for her.

I really would be a fairy, exchanged for the real Brigitte Meidell...

"Undine...," Yuri said reproachfully. But the undine showed no fear and only peered with amusement into Brigitte's dark face.

"You don't know, do you?" she asked.

"Know what?"

"That you're contracted with a—"

Suddenly, the undine shut her mouth.

Brigitte looked at her, confused.

"...Oh, I think you'll learn the name soon enough."

"But..."

"Undine. Don't get her hopes up," Yuri scolded harshly.

The undine puffed her watery cheeks out like a delicate maiden. "You mean to say you don't know, either, master? You disappoint me."

"...What do you mean?"

"That's for me to know and you to wonder."

With that, the undine turned away and dived into the brook. She had probably crossed to the spirit world.

©Yomi Sarachi

Brigitte was so overwhelmed, she couldn't speak for several moments after the undine vanished. What did she mean? Had she meant to poke fun? It was always difficult for humans to discern the intentions of capricious spirits.

"I swear... That spirit." Yuri sighed.

She looked up at him. He was gazing at her face.

"Anyway, did you want to ask me something?" he asked.

"Hmm? Oh yes... Our assignment in spiritology is to demonstrate our communication with our contracted spirit, so I thought I'd get advice from you," she answered, remembering why she'd come in the first place.

He frowned, then moaned, "You think I know?"

...*Good point.*

He was completely right, but she still felt disappointed.

Spiritology class rolled around again before Brigitte could come up with a strategy. Since she didn't have any friends to talk to, she was standing around the training grounds trying to look relaxed while secretly panicking.

The class would take place on the outdoor training grounds, which they'd gotten to by exiting the three-story East Building, where the second-year classrooms were, and cutting through the first-year West Building to the adjacent grounds.

Most extracurricular classes that involved the use of magic took place not in the woods surrounding the academy but on the outdoor training grounds. This was because the careless use of fire magic and the like could easily spark a fire in the forest. In fact, about twenty years earlier, a student had apparently burned down part of the forest in just such an incident. To prevent further incidents, a new training ground was created with a magical barrier erected all around it.

Marjory Naha gazed calmly at the gathered students. The plump spiritology teacher was among the most accomplished mages at Otoleanna Academy.

"Today, each of you will demonstrate your communication with the spirit you have contracted with. Of the five second-year classes, this class will be first to complete the exercise. I have very much been looking forward to today!"

Arghhh...what am I going to do?

Brigitte didn't hear a word she said.

Several people in the Meidell cottage were contracted with spirits. She had been especially eager to talk with the servants who, like her, were contracted with tiny spirits...but none of them had given her any useful advice. After all, communication with tiny spirits was supposed to be impossible. People who contracted with them were able to perform the insignificant little miracles of daily-life magic but only a few times a day. That was one reason why tiny spirits were said to lack a clear personality capable of responding to their contracting human.

Normally, young nobles who contracted with tiny spirits did not even attend academies of magic. Obviously, this was because they would be a source of embarrassment, leading their parents or the children themselves to oppose the idea. In Brigitte's case, though it was clear she would disgrace the family, it wouldn't do for the eldest daughter of an earl, and of the Fire Clan at that, not to attend a magical academy—and so she had been allowed to enroll.

As she fretted, class was moving forward.

One by one, in alphabetical order, the twenty students in the class demonstrated communication with their spirit.

Oh, that salamander's big, round eyes are so cute! That girl with the black hair is contracted with a brownie? Like Carson's sister...

Once it began, Brigitte was enjoying the class so much that she forgot her anxiety. After all, spirits she had seen before only in books were moving vibrantly right in front of her eyes. How could it *not* be fun?

She wasn't the only one. The other students' eyes were sparkling, too, and occasionally a cheer went up. Before they knew it, they were all spectators watching one another interact with their spirits and perform magic.

So that's why he brought all that heavy ice—to make Jack Frost appear. Ooh, how unusual, an ainsel... It's s-so close!

The lovely little fairy flapped its transparent wings, giggling as it flew around Brigitte's head. Being surrounded by so many different spirits was a balm for her soul.

"You're next, Nival. Go ahead," Ms. Naha said.

Nival Weir, the class president, stood up confidently. As his friends cheered him on, he walked to the front of the group—but for a moment, he did nothing. Only after the class was bursting with curiosity did he speak.

"Ms. Naha, there is one student among us who I don't think is fit to be in this class."

Suddenly, the group fell silent. Ms. Naha looked at him reprovingly, but he ignored her and jabbed a finger toward Brigitte.

"Ms. Naha, I think you know that Brigitte Meidell, the daughter of an earl, is contracted with a worthless no-name."

Nival...

Brigitte was so sick of him. She'd had a bad feeling ever since they butted heads two days earlier...but she'd never imagined he would attack her in front of the whole class. Of course, Brigitte knew the moment was wrong to answer him, so she remained silent. She wasn't sure if that was the right decision. Ms. Naha looked at her, nodded slightly, and turned to Nival.

"...Nival, I don't like the term *no-name*. And we are in the middle of class. I would appreciate if you would keep your thought-less remarks to yourself."

"Is it really thoughtless? What I said is true. Everyone else in this class knows it. Am I right?"

As he turned his gaze on the class, students squirmed in confusion. This was somewhat surprising to Brigitte. She had assumed they would all agree with him. But Nival was probably even more surprised. As he looked in confusion from one face to the next, they responded with awkward frowns, not agreement.

Ms. Naha let out a long sigh. "...Nival, I've had quite enough. Please return to your place."

"But...why?"

"You will receive no points. You know why, don't you?"

"What?!"

He was in shock. Ms. Naha turned away, about to call the next student. But Nival stepped in front of her.

"Please, wait! Why am I being punished?!"

Ms. Naha looked at him suspiciously. Apparently finding this outrageous, as he was class president and star student, he waved his arms frantically.

"I...I'm not like Brigitte Meidell! She's nothing but trouble. You should throw her out before me! Why do I have to—?"

"Nival. Please do not disappoint me."

Ms. Naha looked away from him and called the next student. The boy, a friend of Nival's, stood up reluctantly. As Brigitte watched him gloomily...she noticed something and looked up.

Did the wind just shift...?

A second later, her hair was whipping around her face. The other students screamed. Brigitte looked over and saw a spirit looming like a dark cloud behind Nival. A shiver ran down her back.

"An ariel…"

Ariels were second-class wind spirits. Although they were said to ordinarily have mild personalities, they could rage wildly in response to the will of their master. This aspect of their character was so dangerous, it was said to be the cause of certain natural disasters that had destroyed towns and villages. And sure enough, the ariel that had just manifested looked utterly insane. Her invisible arms writhed as if she were trying to gather all the wind in the world. The sky, blue just moments before, was now smudged with gray.

She's whipping up a storm…! But…

The training grounds were ringed by a magical barrier, but that barrier was designed to prevent out-of-control magic from damaging the surroundings…not to protect those inside.

In a worst-case scenario, people could die here.

"Everyone, run!" Brigitte screamed over the raging wind, but most of the students were so terrified, they had huddled face down on the grass.

Only Ms. Naha was staring resolutely behind Nival. Still, she was contracted with sunny little spirits called korpukkur, who hardly had the strength to face down a storm. Even Ms. Naha's own outstanding magical ability might not be enough to halt the ferociously howling wind.

If no one does anything…

She couldn't just give up. She called Nival's name as he stood blank-faced with the storm raging behind him. Hoping at least to protect the other students, she crawled desperately to his feet.

"Nival Weir! Make your ariel stop now!"

"...Brigitte Meidell...you are not fit to attend this celebrated academy!"

The wind howled even more ferociously.

I'm making it worse!

As she watched tearfully, the wild windstorm moved toward her. She could no longer keep her eyes open.

...I'm helpless...

She'd done the opposite of helping, and regret overwhelmed her. She prayed fervently that she would at least be the only one hurt. If Nival had flown into a rage because of his hatred for her, that would at least help her overcome her guilt.

But if Sienna found out I wished for that, she'd be furious. And...

She remembered the breathtakingly beautiful blue-black hair. How funny to think of it at a moment like this. She smiled a little, and a teardrop fell from her eye.

He'd probably tell me he knew I was stupid all along...

Just then, she sensed a flash of brilliant light behind her eyelids. Opening her eyes in surprise, she realized the light was coming from her own chest.

What is this...?

As she wondered, the light grew stronger. The instant it touched the storm emanating from Nival's ariel...the storm vanished without a trace.

"Huh?" someone—everyone, really—gasped in astonishment.

It was no wonder. The roaring gale had been on the verge of swallowing the entire class, and it had dissipated like mist before the light. Even as Brigitte watched this impossible scene unfold, she recalled, as if in a trance, the strange words of the undine.

"You don't know, do you? That you're contracted with a—"

As she realized that the sky was blue again, she lost consciousness.

"...Urg..."

The first thing she saw was a white ceiling. Pulling her sluggish body upright in bed, she realized the medicinal smell filling her nostrils must mean she was in the school infirmary. She had been dressed in a simple gown, perhaps to keep her clothes from getting wrinkled.

Looking down in surprise, she saw that her scarred left hand was still hidden beneath a glove, as was her right. She sighed with relief. She didn't know who had changed her, but she didn't want anyone to see her disgusting old burns.

"Brigitte. You're awake?"

The clean white curtain was pushed aside, revealing Ms. Naha's relieved face.

"Ms. Naha, I..."

"You fainted. My korpukkurs carried you here," she said, sitting down in the chair by the bed.

When Brigitte asked if anyone had been hurt, to her relief, Ms. Naha told her that almost everyone was fine. A few students had fallen in their panic, and flying rocks had hit another in the arm. They had already been treated and returned to class. Brigitte had been sleeping for two hours, and in the adjacent room, Nival was still unconscious after inciting his spirit to violence. Since the point of attending the academy was to learn how to properly use spirits, Ms. Naha thought he would probably be disciplined but likely not expelled.

"It is unprecedented for an out-of-control second-class spirit to be so peacefully subdued," she noted with a sigh. "I'm so sorry you had to risk your life, Brigitte, because I was unable to protect the class."

"Oh, no, not at all... I was sure you would find some way, but..."

Brigitte bowed her head, guilty for having interfered. She had meant only to talk Nival into subduing his out-of-control spirit, but she had provoked it and further enraged Nival.

As she thought glumly about it all, Ms. Naha said, "I'll bet you probably know the nickname for korpukkurs, don't you, Brigitte?"

"...Digging fairies?"

Ms. Naha smiled in confirmation, then placed her finger over her lips. "My digging fairies have secretly built a network of tunnels under this school."

Brigitte stared at her. So they had used the tunnels to stand beneath Nival as he spun out of control?

It makes sense that the academy has some tricks up its sleeve; a spirit could run wild at any moment.

Ms. Naha had contrived a method to neutralize students like Nival without having to do anything herself.

Meanwhile, Brigitte was growing more and more miserable.

"But, Brigitte, it's thanks to you that no one was seriously injured in the incident."

"...It is...?"

"Do you remember that light around your body that negated the ariel's wind?"

She did vaguely remember that. But the spirit she had contracted with would never be capable of such a feat.

There's no way a tiny spirit could stop the magic of a second-class spirit...

She must be misunderstanding something. Did Ms. Naha think that she, Brigitte, had done that?

"I sensed that a wave of spellbindingly beautiful magical power had been conjured," Ms. Naha said. She seemed a bit entranced even now as she remembered it. "It made me wonder, my dear, if you really are contracted with a tiny spirit."

"I don't understand…"

"Perhaps your spirit is simply lazy."

It's just…sleeping?

Just as she was about to ask Ms. Naha a question, the infirmary door slammed open.

"Brigitte!"

Loud footsteps approached. As Brigitte wondered what all the fuss was, Ms. Naha stood up.

"Dear me! I seem to be in the way. I'll be leaving now," she said.

What?!

Before Brigitte could stop her, Ms. Naha disappeared outside the curtain. Brigitte tried to smooth her messy hair and pull down the hem of her simple gown…but before she could do much, the curtain was jerked open again. On the other side, panting for breath, stood Yuri. For an instant, when their eyes met, surprise registered on his face.

"…I heard you fainted, so…," he mumbled in a low voice, as if he was making an excuse for coming. But a moment later, his mouth turned down sullenly as he took Ms. Naha's place on the chair.

Brigitte sighed. What was he going to say?

"…You made me worry for nothing."

"…You…worried about me?"

Brigitte stared at him, bewildered. He stared back at her, equally bewildered. Then he turned away brusquely. "It was just a figure of speech."

"So you weren't worried."

"…I didn't say that."

This is so annoying…

Still…until now, no one other than the cottage servants had ever fretted over her. Never once had a person cared so much that they ran to her side panting, just to see if she was all right. She decided to tell him how she felt.

"…Thank you so much."

"…It was nothing." He snorted. "Anyway, what happened?"

He seemed not to know the details. She hesitated but decided to tell him. When she was done, he said, "I knew you were stupid."

And I knew he'd say that!

It was the same word she'd been hearing her whole life. She clutched the sheets in frustration. Yuri was watching her, his elbow resting on his crossed legs.

"…You didn't have to put yourself at risk. Why are you so reckless?"

Apparently, he didn't literally think she was stupid.

"…Wouldn't you want to do whatever you could?" she asked, pouting.

He looked at her suspiciously. "It's too bad we're not in the same class," he muttered.

"…?"

The casual way he said it, more to himself than to her, struck her as odd, and she waited for him to go on.

"That way I could have stopped that ariel myself."

"…"

She had to consider the implications for a moment before realizing what he meant.

"…?!"

She shoved his shoulder backward.

"…What was that for?"

"…"

Without pausing to worry about his confusion, Brigitte snapped at him, "Please leave."

"What?"

"I'm still sleepy."

He was silent for a few moments.

"You're still sleepy? But Ms. Naha just told me you were asleep for hours with your mouth hanging open!"

"I don't sleep with my mouth open!"

Just leave already!!

She shoved him with all her might, and even Yuri wasn't strong enough to keep from stumbling to the other side of the curtain.

"What's the matter with you all of a sudden?"

"I'm—I'm so tired, I can't suppress my violent impulses! For your own sake, you shouldn't be near me!"

"...I see. Then I'll go back to class."

He retreated with such surprising ease, Brigitte felt a little shocked by her own selfishness. But just after the infirmary door opened, she could hear him muttering at her.

"...I don't understand you... But you had better stop sleeping with your mouth open, or it'll dry out."

I told you I don't sleep with it open!

"...And make sure you don't kick the sheets off, or your stomach will get cold."

I'm not a child!

There was plenty she wanted to shout back at him, but in the end, she said nothing, and neither did he. Only after his footsteps faded did she let out the breath she was holding.

Maybe this was some strange aftereffect of using so much strength. She felt terribly odd.

My face is so hot...!!

The skin burned when she touched it, even though she was

wearing her gloves. Her face was probably bright red. She didn't want Yuri to see her like that...for some reason.

But her heart refused to stop pounding, and her face wouldn't cool down. She tossed and turned on the big bed for a long time.

An hour later, Brigitte changed back into her uniform and returned to class. She had hardly slept at all since Yuri left. The school day must have been long over, because the hallways were nearly empty. She plodded along, leaning against the walls and banisters now and then, still a little sluggish.

She reached her classroom and opened the door without thinking much about it—then froze.

All the students in her class except Nival were sitting in their seats, glum-faced. When they noticed her, they stood, and a few ran over to her.

"Thank you, Miss Meidell," they said in unison.

What is this?

She blinked in surprise. But they kept talking, one after another. She had never exchanged more than a few words with any of them.

"If it weren't for you, Miss Brigitte, I don't know what would have happened!"

"It was so frightening! I thought I was going to die then and there! But at the last minute, a warm light protected us."

"The power of that spirit was amazing. Imagine stopping a raging spirit like an ariel so easily!"

She couldn't get a word in edgewise amid the shower of gratitude and kindness.

"Were you hurt? I'm so sorry. We should have had the courage to step in ourselves."

"And during that test...I should have lent you a pen."

"We were so afraid of getting on the wrong side of the prince and his friends, we couldn't do anything."

When she looked in their eyes, she knew—they weren't lying. As they braved their own shame to tell her how frightened and cowardly they had been, their voices were filled with pain and guilt.

The girl in front of her was weeping openly.

"Miss Brigitte, you're incredible."

The praise was all sincere.

...Now I see.

She had been so frightened of everyone, of being the center of attention. She'd assumed they all hated and despised her...and she'd thought of them all as enemies.

My perspective was so distorted.

She was the one who had shut her heart to the world. She had jumped to the conclusion that they all despised her. Of course, a few of them probably did. But almost twenty students had been waiting on the edges of their seats for her to return.

"I..."

She was about to respond, her voice quivering, when the back door of the classroom opened—and everyone gasped.

As twenty pairs of eyes fell on him, Nival said flatly, "I received permission to get my things."

He doesn't have any obvious wounds...

Brigitte was secretly relieved. But then, to her shock, she noticed something shiny on his neck that hadn't been there before. She had never seen one before, but she was fairly sure of what it was.

A magic-suppressing collar.

The collars both contained the wearer's magical power and confined the spirit that was the source of that power. Serious criminals were made to wear them, and Brigitte had heard they were applied to exiles as well.

Ms. Naha had said she expected Nival to get away without serious punishment—but this was quite severe. Not only would he temporarily be unable to use magic, but everyone would know instantly that he was being punished.

As the whole class stared, Nival walked toward his seat.

...But for some reason, he changed course partway there and turned toward Brigitte.

The other students rose to form a wall between her and Nival, but she shook her head. She was the reason he had lost control to start with.

"...Nival, if you have something to say to me, please feel free to say it."

As his intense gaze fell on her, she met it with defiance.

The students watching held their breaths.

Slowly, Nival began to speak. "I... Th-th-th-tha..."

"...?"

Ththththa...?

Was this some kind of secret code? Nival's eyes darted around; perhaps he had noticed her suspicion. Finally, he said in a voice barely above a whisper, "...Thank...you. You saved me."

Brigitte was stunned.

The other students were exchanging disbelieving looks, too.

Nival wrinkled his nose. "And...I'm sorry I treated you so rudely in the past. I don't think an apology will make it better, but at least let me offer one."

Did he just thank me...and apologize...?

The infamous Nival Weir?

The boy who used to mock her was now bowing at the waist in apology.

Brigitte rubbed her eyes. "Please excuse me. I seem to still be dreaming."

"This is no, uh, dream. I mean it. I feel horrible."

"…I knew it was a dream."

"You have to believe me!"

Nival's forehead was practically touching the ground by this time. Brigitte could hardly tell him she didn't believe him. Still, she couldn't easily accept what was happening.

"…Are you sure this is all right?" she asked, lowering her voice.

He didn't answer.

"If Prince Joseph hears that you lowered your head to me in public—"

"…I know. My family and I might face some sort of retribution. But I lost my future as a royal aide the moment I sent my spirit on a rampage. I'd say that burned my career prospects."

Ah, so this is desperation?

But when he raised his head again, his face was surprisingly radiant. He didn't seem too sorry about the situation.

"That's not all," she went on. "You hated me, didn't you?"

"What?"

"Isn't it humiliating to apologize to someone you hate?"

"I…"

For some reason, he seemed at a loss for words. Finally, though, he admitted she was right, his expression caught between laughter and tears.

"I… Yes, I did hate you."

I knew it.

The truth was, she'd never liked him much herself. But he'd used past tense—which must mean he at least accepted her now.

Still, I never did find out anything about my spirit…

He shouldn't be thanking her—he should be thanking the spirit that erased the windstorm and protected their classmates. But

Brigitte had never heard of any light-emitting, windstorm-eating spirits.

She was more confused than ever. But there was something she wanted to tell him.

"Also, about your ariel..."

"...I'm ready."

Ready for what? she wondered but went on anyway.

"I think your spirit is extremely kind for mirroring her master's anger with her own. I know you won't be able to talk to her while you have the collar on...but please, once it's off, I hope you reward her for her service."

Although I hardly have the right to say something like that...

She was ready for him to snap at her to mind her own business, but instead, he blinked at her in surprise.

"You're...a very kind, strong person, Brigitte Meidell," he said, topping off all the strange things he'd said that day.

"I th-think you must have hit your head, after all...!"

"I assure you, I didn't. And from now on...if you ever need anything, don't hesitate to ask me."

His eyes were almost feverish. She felt like she'd heard something similar recently. Although the person saying them wasn't nearly as earnest.

"I—I want to be of service to you," he said.

Several of the girls nearby squealed.

Brigitte flushed. "Thank you... In that case, I do have one request."

Nival's face instantly brightened.

"Anything, just say the word! I'll do whatever you wish—"

"Really?! Then please let me meet your ariel again!"

"Of cou— My ariel?"

Brigitte nodded eagerly at Nival, who was quite nonplussed.

©Yomi Sarachi

"Yes. The wind spirit who can call storms! I'd never seen one in real life. But I couldn't get a good look this time, and I'd like to observe her more closely!"

Nival sank weakly to his knees as Brigitte realized belatedly that the mood in the room was shifting.

I can't put my finger on it... It's as if they all pity him...

And that uncomfortable warmth in his eyes...

As she was about to ask him the reason, he rasped, "...Of course. I will do whatever you wish."

Brigitte clapped her hands. "You're kinder than I realized," she said.

"...Kind? ...I'm not sure that's the word...ha-ha."

Why is he about to cry now...?

She had no idea what was going on. But before she realized, she was smiling much more naturally than she usually did.

"Your Highness...!"

In an empty classroom, Lisa was clasped in Joseph's arms. Normally, she loved these sweet moments when no one could disturb them. But not today.

She grabbed the hem of his uniform and peered up at him. His handsome face was full of questions, but his expression was gentle.

"What's wrong, Lisa?"

"It's Brigitte Meidell...! In class...she used spirit power to rein in another out-of-control spirit!"

She wondered why he was pretending not to know. Of course he must have heard the story. After all, the whole school was gossiping about it... Did they never tire of talking about her?

Lisa didn't know the details, but it seemed Brigitte had done something to control a second-class spirit that got out of hand. She had stepped forward to protect the other students by trying to bring Nival back to his senses. The rumor had spread, and now everyone was asking if maybe Brigitte Meidell wasn't so useless and haughty after all.

Don't they know the Red Fairy is just a loud, obnoxious nobody?!

Lisa was uneasy. She had a horrible feeling that the tide was turning in Brigitte's favor. But Joseph just patted her head and said listlessly, "...Yes, I heard Nival's ariel got out of control."

His lack of concern was infuriating. She wanted him to understand; she stepped away from him, her lips quivering.

"...I saw it myself."

Joseph raised his eyebrows, silently asking her to continue.

"I saw Sir Nival...acting like he was Brigitte's slave!!"

Nival Weir was president of the class next to hers. He had been friends with Joseph since they were children, and people said he was sure to be Joseph's aide in the future.

He was good to Lisa as well. He had always told Joseph that Brigitte was not fit to be a prince's wife, and she loved to hear it every time. So why was he acting like this?

Lisa thought back to the scene she'd witnessed a few moments earlier.

"He was *smiling* while he talked to her. He was carrying her bag and telling her to mind the step. He was even wearing a collar with a strange pattern on it—just like a dog!"

She rubbed her arm at the unnerving memory, unaware of the actual purpose of the collar.

"Maybe he's acting so strangely because he provoked his spirit... It's so unlike him!" she went on.

Joseph said nothing.

"I mean, Sir Nival is in line to be your assistant! I thought he hated Brigitte—"

"...What are you implying, Lisa?" Joseph finally said. His tone was cool and his face blank. "I'm not as good as Brigitte, so now Nival is bowing down to her?"

...What...?

Faced with this unexpected response, her brain froze.

He didn't like what she was saying—as soon as she realized it, her face went white.

"I—I—I didn't mean that... I'm sorry, Your Highness. I..."

She reached out to cling to him, but then he looked at her hand in disgust. She flinched and withdrew it.

Wh-what do I do now? I've made him angry. How do I fix it...?!

She sniffled, on the verge of tears.

"Come on, Lisa. I'm only joking."

He smiled sweetly at her and took her shaking hand. That alone was enough to calm her shivering and soothe her ragged breath.

"Lisa, think about it. You know Brigitte's just a useless, pushy nobody, right?"

"Yes, Your Highness."

"She might have managed to trick people for now...but that doesn't change the truth. You don't need to worry about vulgar rumors," he announced confidently.

Lisa began to agree.

"Besides, I planned to get rid of Nival anyway. He's nothing special."

"Of course, you're right!"

In that case, she had nothing to worry about.

"There must be something wrong with me," she said. "When I saw that even Sir Yuri seemed to have feelings for Brigitte, I couldn't help worrying."

"…What are you talking about?" His tone was a shade darker, but Lisa was too distracted by his hand twined in hers to notice.

"I don't know the details, but Sir Yuri was having some kind of competition with her."

"Interesting…," he said, although her answer wasn't much use.

"…Yuri Aurealis, eh?"

But Lisa, in her haze of pleasure, didn't hear his low whisper.

CHAPTER 5

She Falls

"…Um, Nival? How long are you planning to follow me?" Brigitte asked, glancing behind her for the umpteenth time.

The muscular boy mincing along behind her, his pace matched to hers, puffed out his chest proudly. The bulky collar around his neck didn't seem to bother him in the least.

"I'll go wherever you do, Miss Brigitte."

Recently, they'd been having this conversation almost nonstop. Brigitte was disappointed by his answer, but he seemed so happy that she couldn't bring herself to scold him outright.

And now he's even calling me "miss"…

For some reason, he seemed fond of her now. He'd originally been a candidate for Joseph's future aide, and she'd thought he hated her…but ever since she'd stopped him from completely losing control in spiritology class, he seemed to feel he owed her something. After the incident, the teachers had apparently questioned him for several days. They'd ordered him to temporarily wear the magic-suppressing collar, although he seemed unfazed by it.

But today, Brigitte was planning to go to where Yuri was—or might be—and Nival's presence bothered her.

"You've come far enough. Would you please leave now?"

"Ha-ha-ha. You don't need to worry for my sake."

I'm not worried about you...

She didn't fully understand it herself, but for whatever reason, she didn't want to bring him with her. As she tried to figure out a solution, she began walking toward the garden by the library...but, at the last minute, decided to go into the library instead.

As he walked through the familiar halls of the brick building, Nival looked around curiously, as if he didn't go in there very often.

Part of her was praying that Yuri wasn't there.

But there he was in his usual seat in the reading area, just where he'd been the first time they met—Yuri, with his glossy blue-black hair and cold citrine eyes. The pale skin that seemed to have never seen the sun, the smooth line of his nose. She should have been used to his good looks by now, but she still couldn't help staring.

"...?"

That was when he noticed her. He glanced up from his book, and their eyes locked. He blinked, shifted his gaze behind her...and widened his eyes.

I knew it.

She opened her mouth to correct his obvious misreading of the situation, but before she could say anything, he muttered his own self-satisfied assessment.

"Is that the spirit you're contracted with, Brigitte?"

"...Not exactly!"

That was unnecessary!

Some misunderstanding! He was unbelievable.

Yuri looked back and forth between the two of them.

"Are you certain? There's something similar about the two of you, so I was sure…"

"Your little joke isn't funny, so can you stop now?"

"I don't joke."

That's even worse!

But as she clenched her shaking hands into fists, Nival was blushing and scratching his head behind her.

"I…wouldn't mind that," he said.

"I would," she muttered glumly.

"Anyhow, Miss Brigitte, what did you need to do at the library?" he asked, oblivious.

"Nothing, I just wanted to see…" She stopped before she finished the sentence and accidentally said something odd. "…I just wanted to see some books, but Sir Yuri is in my way."

"What?" Yuri frowned.

Brigitte became flustered. What was she saying? She should have found a better way to prevaricate.

But Nival, apparently misunderstanding her, nodded eagerly and rolled up his sleeves.

"Got it. Then I'll remove him for you!!"

What?!

Why was this happening?

Brigitte scrambled to grab Nival's arm as he turned toward Yuri.

"Wait! Nival, you don't need to do anything!"

"Of course I do! You just said he was in your way!"

"Oh, I meant…"

She was about to say *something different* but stopped. How in the world could she explain herself?

There's no way I can say I came to see him!

"Excuse me, would you mind keeping your voices down in the library?"

Just then, the librarian with the glasses poked her face around a bookshelf. It was the same woman who always scolded Brigitte and Yuri for arguing in the library. Given how timid she was, Brigitte suspected the other librarians bullied her into dealing with annoying visitors.

Nival wasn't normally a troublemaker, so he turned to the librarian to explain. "I'm sorry, we were just..."

Yuri seized the moment. "...This way!"

"Huh?"

Having crept silently up to Brigitte, he grabbed her right hand from behind. He began to jog, pulling her along with him. She could hear Nival's voice behind them, but Yuri didn't stop. Probably to confuse Nival, he zigzagged among the bookshelves next to the reading area. He clearly knew the library well. Without a single wrong step, he pulled her to the dictionary stacks at the very back of the building, and only then did he stop.

She felt slightly disappointed when he abruptly let go of her hand. At the same time, she realized something.

It didn't even occur to me to shake his hand off...

Yuri turned to her in the dim, dusty space. She couldn't quite read his expression.

"...So, what was that?"

"What?"

"Who is he?"

His calm eyes on her were enough to make her heartbeat quicken mysteriously. She looked away.

"H-he's...the president of my class. Nival Weir, the son of a viscount."

"Don't know the name."

I'll bet there aren't many names Yuri pays attention to...

As she mentally shook her head, he said indifferently, "He's really loud."

"...Yeah."

"Maybe even louder than you."

"Hey, no fair! Even I'm not that nois—"

Suddenly, Yuri propped his right arm lightly against the bookshelf. Pinned between him and the shelf, Brigitte peered questioningly at him. But before she could speak, he placed his left hand over her mouth.

"...?!"

His body covered hers, gently restricting her freedom of movement. Her heart was racing.

"Urgh! Grb—"

"...Keep quiet."

He brought his finger to his lips like he was shushing a child.

As she watched his movements, so close she could have touched him, her breath came to a full stop.

It probably lasted only twenty or thirty seconds at the most. But to Brigitte, it felt like an eternity.

"Miss Brigitte? Miss Brigitte! Where are you?"

"Um, excuse me, but can you please not make so much noise in the library...?"

The sound of clattering feet and voices echoed from two shelves over. But the noisy search party did not find the two of them in their dim hiding place, and after a moment, the footsteps faded again.

After a few more moments, Yuri removed his hand from Brigitte's mouth, and she collapsed weakly to the floor.

"...Brigitte?"

He sounded dubious, but she didn't have the energy to respond. After all...

I didn't realize how big his hands are...
Or how much taller he was than her, when she had always thought of him as slender and delicate. Or the fresh soapy smell he had. Or how surprisingly long his eyelashes were. And everything else.

"Were you holding your breath? Are you all right?"

Do I l-look all right...?

She wanted to scream, but she really was having trouble catching her breath. She couldn't lift her head—and in the end, she said nothing at all.

I've been feeling so strange lately...

It was lunchtime in the cafeteria. Sitting at a four-person table, Brigitte gracefully lifted a forkful of pasta in cream sauce to her mouth. Next to her, Nival, who had ordered a sandwich, was saying something to her...but she was so lost in thought that she didn't hear him.

Yes, something is off.

As soon as school lets out—no, if I'm honest, at all times of the day—Yuri is suddenly on my mind. His expression, his voice, his gestures, his words...every time she thought of them, her face instantly grew hot. To make matters worse, whenever she saw something dark blue or yellow, she instantly thought of his face.

Just yesterday, I made Sienna so worried, she asked me if I'd eaten something bad...

"They were blossoming so prettily, I asked Hans to give us some," Sienna had said, showing Brigitte a vase of blue flowering milkweed. But the blue had reminded her of Yuri. She flushed so hot, Sienna had bundled her into bed then and there... Yes, she really was acting odd.

And the truth was, she knew why.

It was humiliating, but she had to admit it. Most likely...

I'm jealous! I'm jealous of Yuri!

Deciding that definitely must be the problem, she clenched her fists.

Yuri Aurealis. Although he was the fourth son of the Water Clan, he was an unparalleled genius contracted with two—two!—first-class spirits. She had always been aware of him. As the oldest child of the Fire Clan, she had not infrequently been compared to him. And now that they knew each other and talked often, she realized all over again how outstanding he was. Her competitive instinct had been provoked... That must be why she wanted to see him all the time, which only made her even more jealous... Yes, she most definitely had fallen into a downward spiral.

After all...

I heard he was amazing in spiritology class...

After the incident with Nival, students were temporarily forbidden from using the outdoor training grounds. Only yesterday, Yuri's class had finally been able to demonstrate their communication with spirits. She had heard that he had not only engaged in a natural conversation with his undine, but even worse, the pair had unleashed a powerful water spell in midair as the other students looked on in amazement. Brigitte had heard about it from a girl in her class whom she had begun talking to recently.

I wish I could have seen that up close...!

Joseph and Lisa were in Yuri's class—but that aside, she would have liked to be there.

"Blech. Yuri Aurealis..."

"!"

Just then, she heard Nival groan, and she jerked her head up. Yuri himself was standing next to them.

"Sir Yuri..."

"Hey," he answered listlessly, then mumbled, "do you mind if I sit here?"

Nival scowled skeptically. "Of course I mind. Brigitte and I are trying to relax."

"Please join us."

"Miss Brigitte!"

She nodded, having no reason to turn him down, and Yuri sat across from her. She pretended to continue gracefully eating her pasta as if she couldn't care less...

Why, why, why, why did he show up?!

She was secretly in a total panic.

If I'm not careful, I think my hand is going to start shaking the pasta off my fork...! Do not let that happen! He will think you are completely bizarre!

She couldn't help remembering their encounter in the library a few days before. To hide from Nival, Yuri had held her hand. She had held her breath in the dim alley between the stacks where the light didn't reach. Like they were the only two people in the world...

Afterward, she had been so embarrassed, she had rattled off some strange excuse and then escaped.

I swear...

It was like she could still feel the touch of his large hand covering her mouth. Whenever she thought about it, her heart started pounding thunderously and refused to calm down. This was happening daily now. It was becoming a problem.

"So did you want to say something to me?"

"What I'd like to know is why you think I'd have anything to say to you."

As Brigitte looked on silently, Yuri and Nival were sparring curtly. She had to admit that Nival's question made sense, since Yuri typically ate in one of the private booths.

Why had he chosen a table seat today—the very one where Brigitte and Nival were eating? She glanced around. There were plenty of other empty seats.

Could it be because I'm here?

...As she pondered this self-centered notion, she noticed something.

...What's the matter with him?

Yuri seemed to be acting a bit different from usual. She couldn't put her finger on it, but something felt off. She decided to ask him about it while it was on her mind.

"Um, Sir Yuri? Have you been getting enough sleep?"

The dish the waiter brought him held only a small salad. He turned to her without touching it.

"I'm sleeping fine," he said coldly. But his usual sharpness was missing.

If he's not sleep-deprived...is it heatstroke?

She was worried, but she didn't know how to convey her concern. As she fretted silently, he asked, "Why haven't you been to the library since that day?"

She stiffened.

By "*that day*," of course he meant the day she came with Nival. There was no way he could know she'd just been thinking about it, but as he gazed at her, she glimpsed something earnest in his eyes.

"...I...I've had some things to do," she answered vaguely. To hide her shyness, she spread her fan and said, "Aha! Have you missed me, perchance?"

She meant it as a teasing joke, expecting him to reply with his usual outrageous rudeness. But instead, he said, "…I suppose I have."

What?!

She couldn't believe her ears.

He really was acting strange today. Truly abnormal. Even more so than she was.

"Sir Yuri, did you happen to eat some food off the street?"

"No, that's something *you* would do." He snorted.

But he looked so despondent that she timidly held out something from her own lunch.

"…Here, have this."

"What?"

"It's pudding. I thought you'd have less trouble eating something sweet."

Brigitte loved sweets, pudding, of course, included. But she knew when she got home, Carson the pâtissier would give her his latest creation like he did every day, so she could make a lunchtime sacrifice.

Yuri was silent for a while, and she worried she might have overstepped her bounds.

"You're a good person," he finally mumbled.

"Eeep!" she screeched, quaking in fear.

Next to her, Nival let out a frightened "whoa!"

Yuri really isn't himself today!!

She didn't know why—but a few hours later, she learned what had happened to him, by sheer coincidence.

Since he'd admitted to her face that he missed her, she made up her mind to go to the library that afternoon. There were plenty of books she wanted to read. She had some to return, too, although they weren't due yet.

It would be strange to keep avoiding him...

She also wanted to check on him, since she was worried about how he'd acted at lunch. As for Nival, though she did her utmost to convey that he was not welcome, he still insisted on seeing her as far as the library. Now she was standing in front of said library, watching a boy and a girl bicker about something. Brigitte knew them both.

"Sir Yuri, would you join me for a cup of tea?"

"No, thank you."

"You're so smart I doubt you even need to go to the library!"

"That doesn't make sense."

Lisa was complaining loudly as Yuri attempted to walk around her into the library. Visibly annoyed, he tried to dodge her, but Lisa cut him off at every turn.

Inside, the librarian with glasses was walking around in a dither. Brigitte guessed she wanted to scold them for making such a ruckus and scaring off other patrons, but since they were outside, she probably couldn't bring herself to do it.

Even now, a small crowd of students was watching from a distance as Yuri and Lisa argued. Lisa was making no effort to lower her voice, and the sound seemed to be drawing.

Brigitte had a bad feeling as she looked at what passed for a smile on Lisa's face. For the last few minutes, she seemed to have been waiting for an opening of some sort.

No way...

The moment Brigitte guessed what she was after, she stepped forward to break them up. But as she did, Lisa glanced over at her and shouted dramatically, "Even you will pay a price if you go against the wishes of the Third Prince, Sir Yuri!"

Brigitte clenched her teeth. Just as she suspected.

She's trying to trap him publicly...!

Kings choose their vassals, but vassals also choose their kings.

Yuri belonged to an illustrious dukedom, but that was a very different position from the royal family, which was the pinnacle of all nobility. Most likely, Lisa was intentionally tangling with him to point out in public that his attitude was inappropriate.

The watching students were exchanging glances and whispers.

But in contrast to Brigitte's anxiety, Yuri seemed as collected as ever.

"I had no idea."

"No idea? Of what?"

"That the Third Prince was a girl."

Ouch...!

Brigitte's face twitched.

That was just...pure Yuri.

The day Joseph broke off his engagement with Brigitte, he had acted the part of Lisa's affectionate knight in shining armor. But Brigitte still hadn't heard anything about a second engagement. In other words, Yuri was pointing out that right now, Lisa was nothing but a baron's daughter.

Just like last time. He doesn't flinch.

She remembered the last time Joseph and Lisa had confronted him—he'd not only held his ground but retorted with wit and irony.

He acted the same way toward Brigitte, who was as overbearing as they came. Why would he let anyone else—Lisa included—con him into something?

But Lisa just tilted her head in charming bewilderment.

"...A girl? Joseph is most definitely a boy."

"..."

Yuri fell silent in the face of this unexpected response.

Amazing. She didn't back down even when he said that!
Or maybe she hadn't caught his sarcasm—Brigitte had a feeling that was the case.

She'd never talked directly to Lisa. Although Lisa had lied about her the day Joseph ended their engagement, forcing Brigitte into a villainous role, she didn't have many thoughts on Lisa as an individual.

But this time...

Suddenly, Yuri's eyes met hers...but before he could say anything, she acted. She didn't care if he thought she was interfering.

"Miss Selmin," Brigitte called from a distance. Lisa glared sharply at her. Quickly, though, her gaze strayed—as Nival stepped forward to protect Brigitte.

"Nival, please..."

"Don't worry, Miss Brigitte. She's nothing; certainly no match for me," he said, for some reason rolling his shoulders. Brigitte was terrified he might genuinely be planning to knock her out, but Lisa spoke first.

"Sir Nival, you seem to be enjoying that collar your mistress put on you!"

"...What?" Brigitte and Nival said in unison.

Lisa smirked in apparent amusement.

"You're just like a disobedient dog! Although given the kind of mistress you have, I suppose that's only natural."

...Um, is she serious?

She didn't appear to be joking. No—this was a genuine attempt to mock Nival and Brigitte. Nival was silent, perhaps too stunned to find any words. Since he didn't seem to have the energy to answer Lisa, Brigitte took a step forward.

"Lisa Selmin, I don't know what ridiculous idea you've got in your head, but Nival is wearing a magic-suppressing collar."

"A magic what…?"

So she really didn't know what it was. Brigitte went on briskly.

"Check page 136 of the first-year fundamentals of magic textbook."

"…Huh?"

"There's an explanatory note in the right-hand margin."

The real purpose of the shining collar on Nival's neck must finally have dawned on Lisa, because gradually, her face flushed.

"He didn't get that collar from me. Although that should have been obvious."

"…"

"And let me add that because Nival is a diligent young man, the collar is scheduled to come off tomorrow."

"Me, diligent? I'm flattered, Miss Brigitte!"

"Nival, there's no need to cry over it."

"But…how else can I express how deeply I feel?"

"You could also keep it to yourself."

Several people laughed, but Lisa, who until a moment ago had been performing a one-woman show, was not among them. It seemed the students watching them couldn't contain their amusement over the exchange between Brigitte and Nival. But Lisa must have thought they were laughing at her own embarrassing mistake, because her cheeks flushed even redder. She glared fiercely at Brigitte.

"Don't you make fun of me, you worthless Red Fairy!" she screamed, her voice filled with intense loathing.

Red Fairy.

That awful name.

"His Highness abandoned you, you sorry, useless excuse for a person!" she ranted. "I'm the one he loves! Don't you dare talk down to me!"

The air froze. Brigitte stared silently at her.

She might not be able to understand through words.

Still, Brigitte couldn't just let her say whatever she wanted—for Lisa's sake, if not her own.

"Miss Selmin, I—"

But Lisa's next words stopped her mid-sentence.

"Your own father called you a changeling, didn't he?" She curled her lips triumphantly. "Is that why you're not very smart? And that eerie light in your emerald eyes, it makes you look like some sort of demon!"

...Stop.

Her words stuck in her throat.

Don't talk about my father...

Her heart was racing. She grasped her left hand with her right as if to protect the ugly burn scars, but still Lisa went on shrieking.

"How about living up to expectations for once, you good-for-nothing!"

She heard her father's voice attacking her as a child.

As soon as they got home from the contracting ceremony, he had dragged her to the drawing room and shoved her hand into the blazing hearth.

She remembered the sound of sizzling flesh. The agony of it.

She had writhed and wailed, sweat and snot pouring down her face as her whole body grew so hot she felt she would lose her mind.

"Please stop!

"It hurts, you're burning me, please forgive me, please forgive me, Father. I'm sorry, I'm sorry I'm a bad girl, Father, Father, Father..."

Over and over, she had begged for forgiveness. But her father did not release her hand.

In the end, he had hissed, "*This is not my child.*"

I can't breathe...

Brigitte watched in a daze as Lisa went on yelling, now that she'd gotten warmed up, but Brigitte couldn't make sense of words. It was like she was in a dream. A nightmare.

As she stood there in a stupor, she realized something for the first time—something that in the moment, she hadn't had the presence of mind to question.

I wonder why the drawing-room hearth was burning at all when we came home that day.

She shivered.

The chill that ran down her back was so powerful, it took away her ability to think.

She couldn't stay in this dream.

Confused, she looked around. Everything in sight was covered in frost. Brigitte gaped.

How could this be happening? How could the air be so bone-chillingly cold?

...It's summer right now...isn't it?

There was only one person here capable of something like this.

Yuri...?

But she couldn't speak his name. The only thing that escaped her lips was a puff of white breath. Her body, too, felt frozen in place. She shifted her eyes toward Yuri—there was no emotion in his expression.

Unlike when Nival had incited his ariel to violence the previous week, no spirit towered behind Yuri. Yet the air brimmed with his awesome magical power, so strong that it brought everything nearby under its control.

As Brigitte, Lisa, Nival, and everyone else stood frozen, Yuri easily lifted his head and turned his intimidating gaze on Lisa. He was the most beautiful creature in this frozen white world, but his eyes were sharp as knives.

"You fancy yourself the prince's representative? You, a petty baron's daughter?"

His voice was terrifyingly glacial.

Brigitte was shocked. She had never heard him speak like that before.

"......"

Fear sprang to Lisa's eyes. But she could not move, as if her feet were frozen to the ground.

"I thought I warned you that if you interfered with me again, I would not overlook it."

...? Interfere...?

But Lisa herself must have understood because her face was whiter than the chill crawling up her body.

"You've ignored my warning—that must mean you are prepared to accept the consequences."

"...!"

No!

Frost crept over Lisa's feet.

I have to stop him, Brigitte thought.

If she didn't, an irreparable rift would open between Joseph and Yuri—or more accurately, between the royal family and the House of Aurealis. Lisa was Joseph's chosen companion. If Yuri was deemed to have treated her violently, the gates to the bright future before him could slam in his face. Brigitte couldn't stand the thought of it.

I have to stop Yuri...

The other day in class, Brigitte's spirit—at least, what seemed to be her spirit—had wiped out the storm raised by the ariel. But she had been calling her spirit for the past few minutes, and it had not responded. She would have to rely on her own strength.

Just then, she realized something.

I think I can move my hands.

A second later, she knew why.

She always wore white gloves. She used to wear a different pair, but the ones she had now were a gift from the cottage servants to celebrate her enrollment at the Otoleanna Academy of Magic. They were made from materials used by the best adventurers in the kingdom: dragon skin and scales and magical spider thread, said to withstand even fire.

Perhaps they weren't quite fitting for an earl's daughter. Still, the thoughtfulness of the present had made her very happy. She sensed in the gift a wish, almost a prayer, that no one would ever hurt her again. It had touched her deeply.

And now, the protection of those gloves allowed her to move her hands.

Yuri...!

She had no time to think. Taking out an object from its hiding place, she hurled it at him with all her might.

Please don't miss!

And it didn't—it struck Yuri's head.

The object she had thrown was a magic water stone.

Before it could fall to the ground, he caught it with one hand. After examining it, he slowly lifted his head. A vein pulsed at his temples.

"......Hey!"

Uh-oh, he's angry!

"I-I'm sorry! I was planning to give it to your undine as a token of friendship the next time we met!"

"Don't go around currying favor with other people's spirits."

"Oh, there's no need to be so strict!"

Though he remained calm, he was angry enough to frighten her. As she backed away, she realized that her body was free, and she could speak. She looked around and saw the frost that had covered everything in sight was gone.

When her eyes met his again, she could tell he was still irate, but that glacial chill was gone. She let out a long breath.

Thank goodness.

Released from their chilly imprisonment, the other students scattered. Most of them were watching Yuri with fear.

Some bad rumors could come from this. After all, he had manifested his incredibly powerful magic and nearly hurt innocent people in the process. Frustrating as it was, Brigitte knew she'd have a hard time preventing people from talking—even though he had gotten angry in the first place only to protect her.

"Miss Selmin."

Brigitte figured the least she could do was talk to Lisa, who hadn't budged even after the spell was broken. Lisa looked at Brigitte, and the hatred in her eyes seemed to have only grown stronger.

Undeterred, Brigitte kept talking. "I feel very relieved to have spoken to you today."

"…? Why?"

"Prince Joseph told me he likes stupid girls."

Lisa stared at her, uncomprehending.

Well then, I'll make it easier for her, Brigitte thought, smiling. "I'm relieved to see his taste hasn't changed."

"…!"

Incensed all over again, Lisa took in a breath for another tirade against Brigitte. But then, she must have realized she was at a disadvantage because she only said, "…Remember this day, Brigitte Meidell!"

With that, she squared her shoulders and strode away.

"My, my, how rude!" Brigitte sighed, widening her eyes theatrically as she watched Lisa go.

Yuri walked up to her. "I always knew you were mean," he said.

"You're one to talk." Brigitte looked up at him. "…Thank you for protecting me, Sir Yuri."

She bowed her head low.

If Lisa had said much more, Brigitte was sure she would have broken down in tears. Even knowing that was what Lisa wanted, she doubted she would have been able to stay strong.

I hate how weak I am…

Her dejected expression didn't stop Yuri from being his usual self. "I didn't intend to protect you."

"…I suppose you didn't. But I was still happy."

He glanced at her, arms crossed. "…About what?"

"I think anyone would be happy if an acquaintance worried for them."

"…Then go ahead and think of it like that."

He's so irritating!

Somehow, though, she was getting used to his abrasiveness.

"Anyway…what was that all about?" she asked, lowering her voice.

He frowned. "…Can't say. Lately she's been like that all the time," he muttered testily.

"But to change the subject—," Brigitte began.

"You don't care?" he interrupted.

She blinked. She thought he was talking about Lisa's aggression toward him, but apparently something else was on his mind.

"That girl...Miss Selmin...she's your rival in love, isn't she? I saw you watching that time."

"!"

So he noticed me!

Even after all this time, it was embarrassing to admit. But she had something more important to ask him.

"What do you mean, my rival in love?"

"...?" He seemed puzzled. "You like him, don't you? The Third Prince?"

"Oh... Yes, I did care for him."

They had been engaged since they were children, and he had been her only friend when everyone else treated her cruelly. But now that he'd ended their engagement, she saw their relationship a bit more objectively.

I mean, it isn't really right to tell your fiancée you like stupid girls or tell her to wear pink dresses and heavy makeup and pretend to be dumb...is it?

She didn't know why Joseph had done such things. But she guessed that he'd disliked her from the start, or at least from early in their relationship.

I should have noticed that sooner.

"I haven't been thinking much about His Highness lately."

"You haven't?"

"No. I mean, I'm always thinking about you."

...Oops.

Did she just say that? She'd gotten so swept up in the conversation, she might have just made a major blunder. She began frantically waving both hands.

"...O-of course I mean I'm always thinking about my competition with you. You know that, right?"

"...!"

"We tied for first place on the written test...but we're not in the same class, so we couldn't compete on the spiritology assignment! I've been so focused on winning the next round—that's all I meant, because there's no other reason for me to think about you!"

But the more she talked, the more it sounded like she was either lying or making excuses. Heat flooded her cheeks, and there was no way she could stop it.

To make matters worse, Yuri was saying nothing. Growing even more flustered and flushed, Brigitte kept spluttering out flimsy excuses.

"...Ha!" Yuri finally blurted, as if he couldn't contain himself any longer. "Calm down, you silly girl." His eyes were twinkling a little.

"...!!"

She blinked at him, but no sensible words came out. He covered his mouth with a fist and laughed.

I...don't think I'm jealous of him...

That couldn't explain the way she felt about him. It was much warmer than that, but it also ached, and it meant much, much more to her than jealousy. She had never felt this way about anyone before.

I think I...

"I am not a silly girl!"

She looked down, her face burning.

"...I know." His voice was so impossibly kind, she couldn't say another word.

"...Hey! Hey, I'm still frozen! Listen to me, Yuri!"

Behind them, a familiar voice was shouting, but Brigitte's heart was much too full for her to hear it.

CHAPTER 6

The Long-Suffering Attendants?

That night, Brigitte was in agony. She lay tossing and turning on her enormous bed, periodically groaning and gripping her pillow.

She was thinking of Yuri Aurealis and his blue-black hair.

Just the memory of him was enough to make her heart pound.

By all appearances, she was in love.

He's so rude and cold and offensive…even I have to wonder why I like him.

But she knew that although everyone else kept their distance, he was actually a kind person. Everyone hated her, too, but he hadn't judged her based on the bad rumors. He'd listened to her. When she was hurt, he got mad at the person responsible. She always breathed easily when she was with him.

I think I…

"Miss Brigitte?"

"Eeek!"

She leaped up at the sound of the familiar voice. Throwing down her pillow and looking up, her eyes met Sienna's.

"Sienna, please tell me if you're in my room!"

"I did knock."

Sienna, dressed in her usual uniform, sounded unruffled. But Brigitte was startled to see that her eyes were sparkling.

"...Miss?"

"Wh-what?"

"...Nothing, it's just that you've been making so many strange noises since you got home I thought you might be ill."

Brigitte flushed. Sienna was right—she had been making strange noises. She'd also been wriggling her legs around, so Sienna and the other servants downstairs had probably heard her. No doubt Sienna had come as their representative to check on her. Suddenly remembering to be embarrassed, Brigitte looked away.

"...I'm fine. It's just that..."

"Just that what?"

"...Nothing."

This is far too humiliating to tell her...!

She hadn't even told her she and Yuri were friends. How could she suddenly tell her she had feelings for him? She didn't think Sienna would laugh at her, but there were still certain things she couldn't say.

When Brigitte didn't say anything else, Sienna suggested gently, "In that case...why don't you go out tomorrow to cheer yourself up?"

"Um..."

"Just seeing the sights might help your mood, or you could go shopping downtown."

"..."

Brigitte considered this. She didn't usually leave the cottage other than to go to school. The reason was simple. Her parents didn't like it when she went out, so she tried to keep a low profile on the weekends. Since she could ask the servants to buy books or presents for her spirit any time, it hadn't been much of a problem. But the truth was, it was suffocating.

Maybe I will go out. It's been ages...

She gazed up at Sienna.

"Would you come with me?"

"...Me? Don't you have anyone else to invite?"

"I don't have friends."

She was sad to admit it, but she really didn't. Thanks to the incident in spiritology class, she'd grown a little closer to her classmates...but she still had a hard time talking to them. Of course there was Nival, who talked to her every day, but he didn't really count.

"I'm not saying that's the reason, but I'd like to go with you... You're my closest friend, or family member, or..."

"Miss Brigitte..."

Sienna's eyes grew moist. The truth was, she suspected her darling mistress had gotten tangled up with some unsavory man, and she had been hoping that if Brigitte invited him along, she could do some sleuthing—but she could hardly turn down such a sweet invitation. She nodded pertly.

"Of course. I would love to."

"I'm so glad."

"In exchange...will you let me choose your makeup and clothes tomorrow?"

"What?!"

Brigitte was taken aback. Although she'd made up her mind to change after Joseph broke up with her, she still was wearing the same heavy makeup. Sienna was suggesting that tomorrow could be her first step toward something different.

"And why not leave your fan at home, too? You have a habit of covering your face with it any time you don't know what to say or want to hide your feelings."

"...But I'm not sure I'd feel comfortable without it..."

"Using your accessories in that way isn't necessarily bad, but I'd like to see you show more facets of yourself to other people."

Brigitte realized she might have a point. She knew Sienna wasn't just talking to hear her own voice. She truly wanted what was best for Brigitte.

If I become a spiritologist, I'll have to talk to my clients and collaborate with other scholars... I guess I'd better work on my communication skills!

"...All right. I'm looking forward to it, Sienna!"

"Leave it to me, Miss Brigitte."

She wasn't sure, but the diminutive Sienna seemed to be puffing out her chest. The gesture was so adorable, Brigitte suddenly felt much more relaxed.

Argh, I just can't calm down...!

Brigitte stepped anxiously from the carriage after Sienna. They were going out together, as promised. But she couldn't help feeling nervous about wearing clothes and makeup so different from her usual look.

Her long, wavy red hair was hanging in two braids. The hem of her white dress was gracefully wide, making a fresh, sophisticated silhouette. Her makeup was minimal—a little foundation, some bright lipstick, and a touch of pink eye shadow. The look, masterminded by Sienna, perfectly evoked a young lady of gentle birth out on the town incognito.

I suppose I can't relax because I'm so used to wearing gaudy pink clothes all the time...

Thanks to Joseph's tastes, her closet had until recently been stuffed with painful amounts of pink. The weekend he ended their engagement, the servants burned it all. Because many of them were related to the Meidells, many were contracted with fire spirits.

I feel like people are staring at me...

Beneath Sienna's parasol, Brigitte walked nervously along, her long arms and legs swinging. The people they passed—especially the young men—kept glancing at her. She was fairly sure it wasn't her imagination. But while she sensed curiosity, she did not detect malice.

Surprisingly—or maybe not—the people on the streets of the capital did not seem to realize they were looking at the infamous Brigitte Meidell.

"Miss Brigitte? If it's bothering you, let's start a fire."

Just what does she plan to burn...?!

Brigitte was curious, but she decided she would rather not know the answer.

"I'm f-fine. Anyway, is there anywhere you want to go?"

"...Wherever you want to go is where I want to go," Sienna answered. Instead of her usual uniform, she was dressed in a somewhat short light-green dress that suited her extremely well. Brigitte could feel the heat in the glances of men passing by.

"For your sake, I hope I learn fire magic myself soon," she muttered.

"...? I'm not sure I understand, but there's no need for you to burn garbage."

After continuing this muddled conversation a bit longer, they walked by a bookstore and decided to go in.

Afterward, they continued to stroll around the capital. Wherever Brigitte looked, she saw workers using magic. Those with the protection of an earth spirit did construction or public works, while those contracted with a water spirit excelled at plumbing and cleaning. Occasionally, she spotted someone chatting with a spirit that had manifested of its own free will. Simply watching them felt to Brigitte like a good use of time.

What could be better than observing spirits for free?!

She couldn't assume this pastime was as exciting for her companion, however.

"Are you sure about this? You're not bored?" Brigitte asked worriedly.

"Not at all—I'm having fun," Sienna answered. Her expression was as cool as ever, but Brigitte detected a faint smile around her mouth.

Apparently, she didn't mind. Brigitte was relieved, but the summer sun was hot, and she wanted to find somewhere to cool down. Luckily, when she looked across the street, she saw the sign for a magic-stone shop where she often sent the servants.

"How about we go to that shop next?" she asked Sienna, who agreed.

The bell jangled pleasantly as they entered. As she had hoped, it was very cool inside, thanks to the magic ice stones placed in each corner.

Several customers were browsing the merchandise. Because the shop specialized in high-quality magic stones for the upper houses and magic-stone accessories, most were ladies of the nobility.

Brigitte dabbed her slightly sweaty forehead with a handkerchief. As she sighed, she suddenly noticed someone just to the right of her, in front of a display case. As she stepped to the left to get some space, she happened to glance over—and grimaced.

"Yu…"

Yuri?!

She managed to silence herself before blurting out the rest of his name. With both hands pressed to her mouth, she silently scooted to the left. Sienna raised her eyebrows suspiciously, glancing back and forth between the two of them. But Yuri just kept staring down at the polished glass case.

Curse this red hair! Could he really not notice me when I'm right next to him...?

She held her breath, mulling over the situation. Many children in the Meidell family were born with red hair in various shades. Among the cottage servants, Sienna had orange hair and Carson, the assistant cook and pâtissier, was strawberry blond.

But Yuri just muttered to himself, his serious gaze fixed on the shelf.

"Clifford, I'd like...let's see, fifty of the best magic water and ice stones. And ten each of all the others."

"Yes, sir."

Evidently, he was there to buy stones. He was briskly issuing orders to a boy standing next to him who looked around the same age as Yuri and, like him, was handsome and well-dressed. He must be Yuri's attendant. Judging by his light-blue hair, he was likely related to the Aurealis family.

"That reminds me," Yuri went on in the same brisk tone. "I never returned that magic stone the other day."

"?"

"This."

Still not looking at her, he thrust his fist toward Brigitte. Reflexively, she held out both hands, and he set a magic water stone in her palm. The moment she saw the familiar object, she jerked her head up, flushing bright red.

He knew I was here all along!!

What had she wasted all that time worrying for?

If it weren't for the other people nearby, the short-tempered Brigitte would have given him an earful then and there.

Clifford Yuize belonged to a family collaterally descended from the House of Aurealis. His light-blue hair was a diluted version of Yuri's blue-black. Although the rest of his family saw this as a point of pride, Clifford had felt a certain antipathy toward the name Aurealis for as long as he could remember.

After all, wasn't his family like some cheap imitation of the famed Water Clan?

What a miserable business, passing down their thinned-out duke's blood like it was their most precious possession.

Clifford was relieved that, as the second son, it wasn't his task to protect their worthless family, but when his parents told him they hoped he would one day serve the House of Aurealis, he silently cursed his luck.

However, when he met Yuri Aurealis, the duke's fourth son, his feelings changed completely.

If I'd been assigned to serve their second or third son, I'm sure I would have left the city a long time ago...

He felt truly lucky to have been chosen as Yuri's attendant. He was receiving an education he could feel proud of as the attendant of a duke's son. And all of it was thanks to the fourth son of the family he had long hated. Life was unpredictable.

Recently, he'd noticed that Yuri was acting strange. His normally coolheaded, efficient, to-the-point master was more scattered than usual. Sometimes he would stare out the window, lost in thought, or suddenly stop when he passed people on the street.

To top it all off, he had set a completely ordinary magic water stone on his desk and taken to staring at it for minutes at a stretch.

When Clifford had asked him what the matter was, all he got was a cold "nothing." So Clifford left him alone.

His school grades were unchanged, and communications with his spirits were excellent. Nothing obvious had changed in his life. Most likely, his own family members hadn't even noticed he was acting different. As for Clifford, he hadn't been sure whether the subtle change was positive or negative.

But now, as he stood behind his master, he finally knew: For Yuri, at least, this was a wonderful development.

They were at a stone shop that Yuri frequented. The Aurealis family had gone there for generations, and Yuri often ordered magic stones from them to give to his contracted spirits. Sometimes, he also gave his servants magic stones as a special reward.

The servants liked this because when spirits received high-quality magic stones, they often lent their masters potent magical power that improved the efficiency of their work. They had no complaints about Yuri's mindfulness and resourcefulness as a master. Around the mansion, he was feared but respected as a generous young noble.

For some reason, however, this young man who typically had no trouble making decisions had been staring at a single display case for several minutes. Moreover, the case was full of pretty accessories—things a practical man like him should have no use for. Finding this strange, Clifford peered into the case.

Right away, he noticed something odd. His master was not looking at the accessories at all but rather at the reflection of blazing red hair in the glass. When Clifford looked up, he immediately saw who it belonged to.

"Yu…"

The instant the delicate, neatly dressed young girl started to mutter his name, she slapped both hands over her mouth. Then she scooted silently to the left—away from Yuri. She reminded Clifford of a little crab scuttling along the beach—same color, too.

Her red hair was a dead giveaway: This must be Brigitte Meidell, the girl everyone called the Red Fairy.

Having in effect been tossed out of the earl's house, she rarely showed her face in public. Clifford had never seen her in close quarters before, but he detected none of the volatility or foolishness he'd heard rumor of.

…*Now that I think about it…the girls who turn Yuri's head always seem to have red hair…*

No sooner had the thought occurred to him than Yuri briskly issued an order.

"Clifford, I'd like…let's see, fifty of the best magic water and ice stones. And ten each of all the others."

Noting down the order on a form, Clifford glanced at Yuri. He'd guessed Brigitte must be an acquaintance, but Yuri made no sign of striking up a conversation. Did he perhaps not want to see her? The Aurealis and Meidell families were often compared. Although they weren't exactly hostile, the relationship wasn't completely warm, either.

…Or so he had thought.

"That reminds me, I never returned that magic stone the other day."

Aha…

The magic water stone that Yuri handed Brigitte was definitely the one he had been staring at on his desk. So it belonged to her.

But when she took it, her face turned as red as her hair—whether from anger or embarrassment, Clifford couldn't tell.

Now she looks more like a boiled lobster than a crab...

Yuri called over the shopkeeper and asked to buy one of the accessories in the case, and Clifford wrote the unfamiliar item down on the order sheet. When the shopkeeper handed it to Yuri, he passed it straight to Brigitte.

"Here, take this, too."

"...Um, the design is lovely, but..."

"It's nothing special. Just take it."

Uh, that's not true!

Clifford couldn't help silently contradicting his master.

It's worth far more than all the magic stones you just bought combined...!

The silver hair ornament was shaped like a large flower accented by nine small gems, each sparkling with a different color in the center. In fact, it was a magic item of the finest sort, said to ward off any type of magic one time.

Brigitte had to recognize its worth. She hesitated, then peered timidly up at Yuri. "This seems like a gift you should give to a girl who means something to you..."

She sounded so concerned that Clifford nearly burst out laughing. Incredible. Nothing whatsoever had gotten through to her. Yuri was silent for a few seconds.

"...I don't expect to meet anyone like that," he finally said, revealing the tiniest hint of embarrassment.

Oooh. In other words...he means he doesn't expect to meet anyone other than her.

Clifford couldn't believe Yuri had fallen for someone.

But most likely, the only person capable of catching the true meaning of Yuri's misleading words was his longtime companion, Clifford. And sure enough, Brigitte was nodding away.

"Then that's all the more reason to save it for when you do."

"..."

Yuri's face darkened at the imminent rejection. It was all Clifford could do to hold back the laughter rising in his throat.

Oh, these two are hilarious...

As he gripped his sides to keep the laughter in and blinked back tears, he noticed a girl standing behind Brigitte. He could tell by the way she was standing she wasn't just a friend—although she was situated modestly behind Brigitte, she was keeping a constant watch over their surroundings.

She must be her servant-slash-bodyguard...

When their eyes met, she narrowed hers warily. Clifford smiled brazenly at her, and this seemed to remind the sullen Yuri and the slightly confused Brigitte where they were.

"...Let me introduce you. This is my attendant, Clifford."

"This is Sienna, my waiting maid."

Having been introduced by their masters, Clifford and Sienna exchanged greetings.

Just as I thought.

Sienna was the word for an orangish-red color. Her parents must have named her that because they had hoped she would serve the House of Meidell one day. He should know—his own name was a reference to a body of water, a fjord by a cliff.

She's probably thinking the same thing about me right now... A tough position to be in, he thought wryly.

"Sir Yuri, please take this back."

"...I told you, you don't need to give it back. Can't you hear me?"

"Of course I can hear you. And having heard you, I have decided I cannot accept it..."

They're still at it!

Brigitte was yet again trying to hand back the hair ornament, and Yuri was yet again refusing to take it. The other customers must

have mistaken them for a young couple, because they had all slipped out of the shop with indulgent smiles, while the shopkeeper had retreated to the back room. The four of them were the only ones left in the large shop.

Brigitte and Yuri, however, seemed to have eyes only for each other. Clifford was on the verge of laughing again at their complete obliviousness, but Sienna's expression remained prim and proper.

"We both have the hard job of serving eccentrics, I see," he whispered to her.

After a few moments of silence, the cool and collected maid relaxed her mouth so slightly, Clifford thought he might have imagined it.

"...Indeed. And I enjoy it thoroughly," she answered. A laugh escaped Clifford's throat.

But he had underestimated her. The instant Yuri and Brigitte stopped arguing, Sienna interrupted, as if she had been waiting for her chance.

"Pardon me, Sir Aurealis."

"Miss Sienna, was it? Did you want to ask me something?"

"Yes. Would you mind sharing your thoughts on my mistress's appearance today?"

"Sienna?!" Brigitte screeched.

She had probably never dreamed her maid would say such a thing. But Clifford was surprised, too. Not many maids would have the nerve to talk like that to the Frozen Blade; given most people found him so intimidating, they shunned him altogether.

This is no ordinary woman...!

As far as he could tell, Brigitte seemed like quite an interesting girl, and he decided the same went for Sienna. Although he didn't realize it, she was older than him.

As for Yuri, he seemed embarrassed by the maid's sudden

request, but since he was essentially an earnest person, he did not snap at her.

"Wh-what…?" Brigitte asked, her voice cracking and her cheeks flushed. She began pawing through her purse but then stopped as if she'd remembered something.

…? Did she forget her fan…?

His guess was correct. Now that her most crucial accessory had been confiscated by Sienna, Brigitte was in a panic at not being able to hide her face. Even to Clifford, her pure beauty and dainty bashfulness were extremely attractive. But of course, Yuri would never say something so sweet.

"…It's not bad."

Ah, well. I suppose that's the best he can do.

Really, extracting any comment whatsoever from a person so uninterested in girls—in other human beings—was an impressive feat.

Clifford nodded, satisfied with this response, but Sienna kept prodding. "Can you please be a bit more specific?"

"…"

Yuri was silent. He probably hadn't expected to try again. Clifford wondered if he should rescue him. At the same time, he was curious to see how Yuri would extract himself from this bed of thorns.

It was the only time Clifford had ever regretted being an attendant guarding his master's back—because it meant he couldn't see Yuri's face.

"I think she's pretty…today and every day," he managed to mutter after a heroic mental struggle.

"Eegya!"

Brigitte leaped backward with a kind of strangled yelp.

"Is that so?" Sienna asked with cool pride.

I suspect that was meant to be praise for what he said...

Maybe he was imagining it, though.

Sienna walked over to the utterly flustered Brigitte and whispered loud enough for him to hear, "Miss, would you like to chat with the gentleman after this?"

"Wh-why would you think that?! I came here today to spend time with you. I don't have even the slightest, tiniest intention of spending time with Sir Yuri!"

"Oh, I see. I assumed you arranged to meet him here."

"Of course I didn't! Of c-c-course not!"

Miss Brigitte's voice is so loud, I can hear every word...

She was by now so worked up, he thought she might develop a fever. This was a bit concerning. Evidently having reached her limit of humiliation, she dragged Sienna over to Yuri and glared defiantly up at him through teary eyes. The image reminded him of a small animal threatening a bigger one.

She probably had no idea how adorable this was.

"Sir Yuri, I will see you the day after tomorrow. Have a nice day!"

"Right... Don't trip over the stoop."

"...I am not a child!"

Sienna nodded at them as Brigitte dragged her away and huffed out of the shop. Clifford watched them go...then turned to see how Yuri was taking this.

The face of his young master, who had spoken more words today than ever before, was completely empty of emotion.

"You should have told me you were close with the Meidell girl."

"Do we look close to you?"

"Yes, very."

Yuri sighed tiredly. But Clifford noticed that in all the confusion—Yuri had succeeded in giving her the present.

As soon as the bell rang to signal the end of class, Lisa jumped up from her seat. If she didn't hurry, the girls would leave before she had a chance to talk to them. But when they saw her walking up, their faces clouded over. Lisa pretended she didn't notice.

"Would you like to join me for tea today?" she asked brightly.

The three girls exchanged glances.

"Um, no, thank you."

"I'm sorry, but I have to do something."

"So do I…"

Smiling apologetically, the three of them stood up and hurried out of the classroom. Lisa watched them in a daze.

"…What is going on?" she mumbled.

They had always relied on her for everything. Without her, Prince Joseph's favorite, they would never have so much as exchanged a word with him. Her influence was the reason they got to enter the private cafeteria booth that normally only high nobles used. And now they were biting the hand that fed them! Lisa's fists quivered with incredulous anger.

…But she knew why it was happening.

They were distancing themselves from her because of the incident last week.

Lisa had angered Yuri Aurealis, the much-feared Frozen Blade. People were still whispering about it, embellishing the story with each retelling. She'd overheard people criticizing her for her recklessness in challenging the Water Clan. Furious, she had lashed out at anyone she caught talking behind her back, but that did nothing to ease her irritation.

What was even more unbelievable was how Yuri had acted that day. People kept their distance because he was so exceedingly good at everything. At the same time, just about every girl in school had an eye on him thanks to his good looks and good family. No matter how much he pushed them away, plenty of girls were still plotting their way into his heart.

And yet this very same Yuri had protected Brigitte. It was incomprehensible.

Why in the world would he care about that worthless Red Fairy? She couldn't imagine a less suitable partner for him. Brigitte's own father had called her a changeling. The Third Prince had dumped her. The whole school made fun of her...so why had the gifted duke's son chosen her?

She hasn't made half the effort I have to be lovable!

Unlike Brigitte, Lisa had put her all into this. She had contracted with a spirit who had a name. She had befriended the rather lonely Prince Joseph and healed his wounded heart. She was the one who had rescued him after Brigitte wore him out. Brigitte ought to get down on her knees and apologize to Lisa for all the trouble she'd caused the prince when she was his fiancée. She truly felt that way. But Brigitte's words kept echoing in Lisa's head.

"Prince Joseph told me he likes stupid girls. I'm relieved to see his taste hasn't changed."

She bit her lip so hard, she drew blood.

I will not stand for it! I'll make her pay!

Stealing pens was child's play. This girl required a much harsher punishment. Otherwise, she would probably never understand what a worthless, classless human she was.

The more Lisa thought about it, the more excited she became. Just the idea of the wounds she could inflict sent a thrill down her spine.

She looked so hopeless when I mentioned her scars...!

Her father had burned her hand, damaging her forever. What

hideous wounds must be hidden beneath those unladylike gloves of hers?

It'd be so fun to expose them in front of everyone.

Now in excellent spirits, Lisa noticed that her dear prince was about to leave the classroom.

"Your Highness! Where are you going?" she called playfully.

He turned and smiled slightly. "I have something I need to do today."

"Oh…"

Joseph was a member of the royal family. Although he'd told her he was excused from most duties to focus on his studies, he must still be very busy. Convinced that this explained the situation, she smiled brightly at him.

"Shall I come with you to the royal palace?"

Having her along would surely calm his nerves. Plus, if she was lucky, she might even get an audience with the king or queen. Joseph hadn't made a move toward engagement yet, saying it was still too soon after his breakup with Brigitte.

But he shook his head. "No, I'm fine. See you tomorrow."

Before she could answer, he left the classroom. Sadly, she watched him go.

…For some reason, she felt like she could hear Brigitte's voice lecturing her again.

"Prince Joseph told me he likes stupid girls."

But that can't be!

The first time Joseph talked to her, he had complimented her for being smart. He'd told her how different she was from Brigitte.

I did everything for him…

It never occurred to Lisa that her feelings might be warning her that something was wrong.

CHAPTER 7

The Magic-Stone Hunt

"Miss Brigitte, will you be my partner in the magic-stone hunt?"

In the hushed classroom, Nival held his hand out to Brigitte, almost like a challenge. She shook her head.

"I'm sorry."

A buzz went through the room while her classmates gaped at Nival with open pity. But he paid no attention, instead staring wide-eyed at Brigitte.

"You're not going to be partners with *him*, are you?"

"Who do you mean?"

"Of course I mean Yu—"

"I do not intend to be partners with anybody!" she interrupted before he could utter the dreaded name. She unfurled her luxurious fan, which Sienna had returned, and laughed haughtily. "I am aware that some people work as a team…but I wish to rely only on my own ability."

After her neat and clean look the past weekend, she was playing the villainess with more dramatic flair than usual, but her classmates were so used to it that they didn't even notice. As for Nival, he seemed disappointed but not surprised.

"That makes sense... With your ability, I'm sure you'll be fine alone..."

Uh...I'm not so sure about that...

Brigitte didn't say what she was thinking, however. Her spirit had stopped Nival's ariel from going on a rampage, but even though Brigitte had been trying to talk to it ever since, she'd gotten no response. She didn't have much hope of getting help from her spirit this time around, either. What she did have was confidence.

As a future spiritologist, I am determined to win...!

Everyone in class was talking about the magic-stone hunt. Officially, it was the practical portion of the upcoming exams. The challenge was to collect special magic stones hidden by the teachers in the dense forest surrounding the academy. All students took the test before summer vacation in their second year, making it something of a school tradition.

Success demanded that students at the very least get help from their contracted spirits—and more importantly, that they grasp the movements of wild spirits not contracted with anybody.

Although spirits basically spent their days in the spirit world, some of them emerged from time to time in sacred, sparsely populated parts of the human world, such as forests, groves, and rivers. The forest around Otoleanna Academy was one such place that they favored. And because spirits universally liked magic stones, they tended to carry off the ones that teachers scattered around for the test.

The test lasted two days. Students were required to spend one night in the forest. This was a daunting requirement for the sons and daughters of nobles, so many students formed teams for the test.

Causing direct harm to either students or spirits was forbidden, and the permitted equipment was defined in detail.

The challenge was to propitiate as many spirits as possible in a short time—in other words, to win their favor so they would gift their magic stones.

And since scores were based simply on how many stones each student received, Brigitte couldn't help feeling eager for the test.

That day after school, Brigitte went to the gazebo near the library.

"Sir Yuri!"

Yuri, who was reading a book, looked up. When she sat down across from him, his well-shaped eyebrows furrowed together in puzzlement.

"Back to your old self, I see?"

"...Yes. I was just experimenting...I suppose."

A shadow passed over her face. Yuri had to be referring to two days ago, when they'd run into each other downtown. Her makeup, clothing, and hairstyle had all been different from usual, and to make matters worse, Sienna had said some mortifying things. It was awful. Not to mention what he'd said in return or the present he'd given her. She still hadn't made sense of it all.

I couldn't sleep all weekend... Ugh, enough.

She had to stop. Thinking about it was likely to give her a fever. She was about to change the subject when Yuri spoke up again.

"You're not wearing it?"

"What?"

"The hair ornament."

I've been trying so hard to forget about that! She glared at him reproachfully.

But he met her gaze with his, which made her so flustered that she had to look away.

Please don't blush...

Praying that her recently disobedient cheeks would listen, she mumbled an answer.

"...I-I'll wear it if I feel like it...but I really should give it back to you, shouldn't I?"

The day he gave it to her, she'd said over and over that she was giving it back, only to discover it in her hand after fleeing home in a panic—although Sienna seemed to have known all along that she had it.

She knew the ornament was incredibly expensive. She also knew it wasn't a gift for a girl viewed as a heretic by her own family.

But instead of answering her question, Yuri made a request. "I wish you'd wear it as often as possible."

Huh?

She was astonished, but his expression remained blank. It seemed he would not drop the subject until she agreed. She had no idea how to respond. Honestly, he was telling her to wear the present he himself had given her? It was almost as if...he felt something for her. She couldn't help wishing that was true.

B-but...I know that can't be right!

Attempting to hide her roiling emotions, she answered defensively—although her high-pitched voice hardly hid anything.

"Ah-ha-ha. Forgive me, but I only wear accessories that I like."

"You didn't like my present?"

"No, I didn't...mean that. It's lovely, and the workmanship is beautiful..."

"Ah. Then please wear it."

She'd been trounced.

"...If you insist...I'll wear it starting tomorrow." She hugged her bag.

I can hardly admit now that I've been carrying it around with me...!

She pressed the handle, hoping he wouldn't guess she had it with her.

Yuri glanced at her hand and shut his book. "And? What did you want to ask me?"

"About the magic-stone hunt, of course."

He nodded. He must have guessed she'd say that.

"Considering my spirits will be helping me, I'll have an advantage... You don't mind?"

"If anything, that should balance the odds. After all, I'm a spiritologist in training," she declared boldly. He seemed to catch her meaning.

"You're confident you can communicate with wild spirits, eh? I still think I'll win."

"Ha! I'm looking forward to seeing you cry when you lose."

"Your confidence is really something. But if you want to waste time dreaming about victory, I don't mind the advantage."

"Aren't you the one with a penchant for dreaming of victory?"

They scowled at each other.

They had tied for first place on the previous written test; this magic-stone test would settle the score once and for all.

"So whoever gets the most magic stones wins?"

"Yes. And like last time, the loser has to do one thing the winner says?"

"Excellent."

He laughed softly—or she thought he did. She threw him a defiant glance.

I'll beat him hollow this time!

It was the morning of the magic-stone hunt. Brigitte, dressed in the designated short, comfortable clothes, was stretching as she waited at the forest entrance for the test to begin. The sight of a hundred or so second-year students gathered there, all dressed like her, was quite a spectacle.

Some were standing in teams of four or five while others, like Brigitte, were alone. As for her few acquaintances—Yuri, one class over, was also standing alone at a distance from the other students. Her heart leaped when their eyes met briefly…but she quickly looked away.

I have no reason to do that!

She glanced at him again. To her disappointment, he was focused on the forest now. Since he'd made such a fuss about it, she was wearing the hair ornament on her ponytail.

No, I'm wearing it because it's an excellent magic item— that's all.

She looked around, trying to regain her mental peace. Although everyone was dressed nearly identically, some students or their spirits were carrying heavy-looking packs most likely stuffed with sleeping bags, clothes, and food. Anyone who left the forest would be automatically disqualified. They had likely overpacked knowing they would need to spend the night in the forest. Brigitte, on the other hand, had only a small knapsack.

I'll have to move around a lot. I don't need all that extra stuff!

She had barely managed to escape Sienna, who insisted she take lots of spare clothes.

"Um…"

Huh?

Hearing someone call her, Brigitte turned around.

"Miss Brigitte!"

But she was distracted by Nival, who came striding over, waving eagerly. Everyone stared at them. The sight of the boy who Prince Joseph had been grooming as his aide chasing after the prince's ex-fiancée must have been quite a shocking sight.

"You seem very energetic, Nival."

"How could I not be? I was so excited to see your performance today, I couldn't sleep!"

With his magic-suppressing collar removed, Nival himself was expected to perform well, but when she looked closely, she saw that his eyes were bloodshot. She was worried.

"Nival…it won't be quite as hot in the forest, but it's still summer. Make sure you rest, all right?"

"I am honored that you are worried about me, but I'll be fine. I'm determined to win even without you by my side!"

Brigitte blinked.

He's going it alone?

She looked around. For some reason, their classmates were standing apart from one another. They all seemed to be watching her with a terrible excitement in their eyes. As she wondered what was going on, Nival explained.

"When you said you were going to rely only on your own ability…we were all inspired to do the test solo, like you."

"What?!"

What in the world? She hadn't heard a word about that.

Nival raised his fist triumphantly in the air. "It's time to show the other classes how amazing you are!"

What?!

The starting bell rang. Thanks to him, she began the test a few seconds late.

Physical fitness, magical ability, negotiating skill—and luck. Of the four elements crucial for the magic-stone hunt, Brigitte felt confident about two: physical fitness and negotiating skill.

But the other two I have none or less of…!

Brigitte Meidell was not a person who relied on anything so hazy as luck. As her classmates scattered, she made her way into the dense forest at a leisurely pace. Fortunately, they had nearly two days to complete the test. There was no reason whatsoever to panic at the starting bell. The air in the shadowy forest was a little humid, but what she noticed more than that was a kind of buzz that tickled her back. In all likelihood, it was coming from spirits dancing with joy as they discovered the special magic stones and tucked them away in their arms or wings or perhaps even secret treasure boxes.

Let's see, where was it? …Aha!

She found the oak tree she had been looking for. She plucked three leaves from the tree, whose flowers reminded her a bit of hairy caterpillars. She was rolling up the verdant leaves with practiced motions when she noticed something.

…Who's there?!

She sensed someone or something behind her.

Directly harming another student or a spirit during the test was forbidden, but in the past, certain students had taken advantage of loopholes to harm their competitors.

Brigitte hid behind the oak tree and held her breath. But as soon as she saw the face of the person who appeared from the bushes, she relaxed.

"Sir Yuri."

"! ...Oh, Brigitte."

He appeared to have been searching near her by chance. He seemed surprised but quickly regained his composure.

"How's it going?" she asked him.

"Just one so far."

"What?!"

He was holding a sparkling magic stone in his hand. She was flabbergasted. The test had just begun!

Never underestimate him...! She gritted her teeth.

"You?" he had the nerve to ask.

"...Zero," she muttered, overwhelmed by frustration.

"Ah. Hope you find one."

"Of course I will!!" she snapped.

"Be careful," he said over his shoulder as he walked away.

"I'll be fine. Don't forget I'm a future spiritologist," she said as she left.

She didn't notice the melancholy glance he cast over his shoulder.

"Ohhh, a stone? You mean this?"

"You want this stone?"

Two tiny fairies in silky white dresses were fluttering around Brigitte's shoulders. Each had her arms wrapped around a magic stone, which looked enormous next to their delicate hands. Brigitte smiled back nonchalantly. As the chatty silkies stared at her with their big eyes, she gave a dramatic nod.

"Yes. I want you to trade me those stones for these flutes."

She blew into the leaf whistle in her hands. At the sound, the silkies twirled in excitement.

"Why does it make a sound?"

"Why is the leaf crying?"

"This is a magic leaf. I asked it to cry for me."

The silkies nodded, evidently convinced.

"I'll give you my stone."

"So will I."

"Thank you. I will make a leaf whistle for each of you."

They completed their trade, and the silkies flitted around, fiddling curiously with the rolled-up oak leaves Brigitte had handed them.

"When you blow it, squeeze one end of the tube. But make sure you leave space for air to get through."

She wasn't sure if they heard her as they flew away. She sighed. Silkies were known for their upfront nature, and this was the third time in a row she'd made a successful trade with them. She now had five magic stones in the pocket of her backpack.

I may have reached my limit of silky trades… Considering how much those little fairies love to gossip, the value of noisemaking leaves might soon fall.

The magic stones she had obtained were decorated with a delicate fairy-wing pattern inside them. This was the emblem of Otoleanna Academy, and to inscribe it on the outside, let alone the inside, of a magic stone required skill both as a magical artisan and as a craftsman. Because the stones were imbued with the vibrations of the artisan themselves, they were virtually impossible to forge.

These were the stones the students were competing for. As the sun shone down from high overhead, Brigitte wondered how she was doing compared to everyone else. She had seen students from other classes several times, but given her unpopularity, no one had approached her, so she'd had no chance to pick up information.

I can't imagine I'm doing too poorly...

She stood thinking for a moment. When Yuri had interrupted her in the process of making leaf whistles, he already had one magic stone. No, she'd better not get too confident.

"Pull yourself together and focus on doing the best you can!" she said out loud to motivate herself.

What should her next strategy be? She was fairly sure she knew more about the various types of spirits and fairies than anyone else. Although stories typically depicted spirits as serious and fairies as cunning, both were straightforward in their own way. Spirits were honest and sincere toward humans, while fairies liked to play with them thanks to their forthright curiosity and mischievousness.

That's why I like spirits.

They seemed so much better than humans, who were full of dirty tricks. Although she couldn't rely on help from her contracted spirit, the one overwhelming advantage she had over other students in this test was her ability to negotiate based on her knowledge of spirits. She was determined to draw on everything she knew to find a path to victory.

In terms of which fairies would be most drawn to magic stones— coblynau, the mine gnomes, seem like a good bet... I think I'll head a little farther into the forest. Although I'd really like to search along the riverbank as well...

She imagined Yuri and his undine had probably already scoured that area for magic stones, however. It would be best to avoid another encounter with him if she could.

I won't let him beat me, though. I just don't want him to distract me!

Reciting puzzling excuses to herself as usual, she continued down the slope she was standing on.

It was pure coincidence that she heard the scream.

"Ahhh!"

It sounded like a girl around her own age. The very faint cry had come from deep in the forest. Without thinking, Brigitte swung into action. She tucked her sixth magic stone, which she had just dug from between some tree roots, into her knapsack.

As far as the test goes, it might be wiser to pretend I never heard that...

She should probably take it as a sign that she had one fewer rival. After all, since demons had been removed from the forest, there was no real threat to anyone's life. But she knew some spirits didn't hesitate to hurt humans, which made it hard to ignore the scream.

"Is anyone there?" she shouted as she walked in the direction of the voice, but there was no answer. Was the girl farther away than she'd thought? She searched for any sign of human presence.

There are too many footprints to tell which ones are hers. If only a spirit would appear...

If the girl had a contracted spirit, it would likely send out some sort of call for help. Frustrated, Brigitte kept walking. Just then, she heard the scream again. Squinting through the unchanging vista of trees, she noticed a small white form floating in the air.

It's a...

The moment she realized what it was, Brigitte started running.

"Please don't follow me!" the girl was screaming.

When Brigitte reached her, she shouted, "Stop!"

Although the girl's momentum carried her a little farther, she finally stopped. At her feet was a round little fairy with an angry face, but it did not attack Brigitte.

"It's all right. I'm here to help you. Can you tell me what happened?" she asked as calmly as possible. But the girl, whose eyes were swollen from crying, appeared to be in shock.

"Wh-wh-why...?"

"Your contracted spirit, the brownie, was throwing pebbles over its shoulder, right? That was a sign."

"..."

For some reason, the girl shook her head. It wasn't a logical response to Brigitte's question, but she didn't have time to worry about that.

"What are you running from? I don't see anyone behind you."

"I... Um, there's no one there, but I think someone is following me..."

The girl was a classmate of Brigitte's named Kira, and she seemed to be at her wit's end. She glanced over her shoulder, her black hair swinging. Brigitte followed her gaze. But just as Kira had said, there was nothing behind them but eerily rustling trees.

"Did you look behind you lots of times?"

"Y-yes. Over and over. No one was ever there...but I felt them watching me. I swear!"

She peered at Brigitte from between her long bangs, as if to say *Please believe me*. Brigitte didn't think she was lying, of course. The agitated state of her brownie, a normally mild-mannered spirit, was another clue that Kira's fear was real.

Brigitte pondered the situation. *Maybe...*

She gestured for Kira to listen. Hesitantly, the girl brought her face close to Brigitte's.

"...Kira, can you please take your clothes off?" she whispered.

"...What?!"

Her eyes widened. For some reason, they were welling with tears.

"Are you angry about what happened before...?" she asked.

What happened before?

Brigitte had no idea what she was talking about. But if Brigitte's hunch was right, taking off her clothes wouldn't be enough.

"Actually, not just your clothes—your shoes, too."

"My shoes?! Are you going to throw them in the river...?!"

"...! Of course not. I'll take mine off, too. Brownies don't wear clothes, so yours are fine."

"Um...?"

Kira stood frozen and uncomprehending, her mouth hanging open.

"I know I said to take them off, but all you need to do is turn your clothes front to back and put your shoes on the opposite feet. Can you do that?"

"Um...I..."

"I'll do it first. Will you trust me?"

Brigitte wanted to laugh. Who would trust advice from the Red Fairy, the dunce of Otoleanna Academy?

But Yuri trusted me...

He never questioned the truth of what she said. He teased her and made fun of her, but he knew she never lied. He probably had no idea how happy that made her. And it wasn't just Yuri. Nival and the other students in her class believed in Brigitte—and in her spirit. They were even grateful.

Because that truth was etched into her memory, Brigitte walked to the shadow of a tree and began undressing without a moment's hesitation. Fortunately, she wasn't wearing a dress, so she was able to change without the help of a maid.

Finally, Kira snapped out of her daze and made her way to the shadow of another tree to begin changing. For a few minutes, the only sound was that of rustling clothes.

"...Done!" Brigitte said, squeezing Kira's left hand. Her thin shoulders flinched.

"Uh, um...?"

"I'm going to run a ways, Kira. Can you follow me?"

"...Yes!"

Brigitte nodded, then took off running, pulling Kira along. It was hard to run with her shoes on the wrong feet...but she didn't slow down. Kira kept pace so she wouldn't lose hold of Brigitte's hand, and Brigitte was relieved to find she had more stamina than her appearance would suggest. Her brownie followed at a slight distance.

The three of them kept running until they finally burst out of the dark, dense woods. Only then did Brigitte stop. She dropped Kira's hand and glanced back. She was panting, her shoulders heaving.

"Good job. That wasn't easy," she said, handing her the water bottle she'd taken from her knapsack. Kira thanked her and took a gulp while her brownie flew around her feet in protest. Brigitte signaled with her eyes, and Kira set the bottle on the ground a slight distance away, then returned without glancing back. Brownies tended to run away if they received direct thanks or payment. The small spirit picked up the water bottle and ran off with it.

"Um, Brigitte? Why did we do that with our clothes and shoes?"

"Because a leshy was after you," Brigitte answered, reversing her clothes again. Kira stared at her. She must not have heard the name before. But it had been her own comment about turning around with no one there that tipped Brigitte off to the spirit's identity.

"It's a kind of fairy that leads people astray in the forest. Most travelers who never return home are said to be the victims of leshies. If you turn your clothes around and put your shoes on the wrong feet, they become confused and can't follow you."

"Wow..."

Kira must have realized the danger she had been in because her face went white. If she had gone on screaming and running around at random like that, it could have been hard to rescue her.

I'm glad I got there in time...

Brigitte sighed in relief. Just then, she heard water falling.

"It's raining..."

She looked up as raindrops spattered her cheeks. They must have been running around in the woods for a long time. The sky had been blue when she had started, but now it was covered in storm clouds. Even as she stood there, rain was drenching her head.

"Uh, hmm...," Kira said just as Brigitte was thinking they'd better find some shelter.

She was pointing at her brownie, who was hopping cheerfully toward the entrance of a small cave.

Brigitte and Kira stepped into the cave the brownie had found for them—although it was more of a hole in the rocks than a cave. Inside, it was warm and a bit humid but not unpleasant. The entrance led to a space surrounded by rough rock walls. Brigitte gazed at the hazy view outside the cave. The rain was coming down harder, and she could hear thunder in the distance.

If I don't want to wear myself out, I'd better rest here for a while.

The fact that her clothes were still nearly dry was one bit of good luck in all this.

"The storm's getting worse. Let's rest here."

"All right!" Kira answered, her voice cracking.

They put their bags in a corner of the cave, and Brigitte took a small magic earth stone from the outside pocket of her knapsack.

"Kira, can I give your brownie a present?"

"Yes, of course, but is that magic stone…?"

"Oh, no, I brought this from home."

She'd set it aside before the hunt, thinking she might be able to use it when negotiating with spirits, but all the spirits she'd met so far had refused to trade a "patterned stone" for an "unpatterned stone"—they could sense the greater power in the former.

The brownie, a cleaning fairy, had produced a broom and was briskly sweeping the cave. Brigitte buried the magic stone in a corner, doing her best not to look at the brownie. Kira watched her curiously.

"*Huff, puff…*"

The little spirit, no taller than a child, went on intently cleaning the cave, oblivious to Brigitte's fascination. *What an adorable creature.* Her shoulders began to shake with suppressed laughter. She used to dislike little spirits like brownies, but she was tickled by the sight of this one happily cleaning.

"You're such a cute little thing, rolling around like an acorn! Yee!"

"Did you just say '*Yee*'?"

Oops!

She'd completely forgotten about Kira. Practically fainting from embarrassment, she desperately tried to cover up her slip.

"You must have imagined it! Ah-ha-ha, maybe it was the sound of thunder…"

It's painful to hear myself!

But Kira just nodded solemnly and said, "Yes, you're probably right."

Brigitte turned her back on the brownie and sat down facing the rock wall. Kira sat next to her, leaving a few feet of space between them. For a while, the only sound was that of the brownie walking around the cave, sweeping.

"I was wondering, Miss Brigitte. How do you know my name?" Kira finally asked.

"We've been in the same class since last year!" Brigitte smiled with chagrin. How rude would she have to be to still not know it?

"...Um, you must have...heard about me, right?"

"What do you mean?"

"He didn't..."

He?

Brigitte remembered that Kira had said something strange when they had first encountered each other in the woods. She glanced over. Kira was staring at the floor, her long bangs covering her eyes almost completely. She wondered what to say, then decided to be honest.

"I'm sorry, I have no idea what you're talking about."

"...Oh yes, of course..." Kira was hugging her knees and rocking back and forth. Brigitte did not prod her. Finally, in a shaky voice, she said, "I'm so sorry...I never told you. I..."

Brigitte listened as she continued, making the appropriate sounds now and then. When she was finished, Brigitte asked, to be sure she understood, "...So you were the one who stole my pens?"

"...Yes. I'm so sorry."

"Thank you for telling me the truth."

"I deeply regret what I— Huh?" Kira stopped shaking and looked fearfully up at Brigitte. "...That's a-all? You're not angry...?"

"What's the use in that? That test's over."

And Yuri even admitted that I tied him for first place...

Anyway, before that test, she'd always scored near the bottom of her class. Compared to that, scoring in the top third was still impressive.

"You could turn me in to the teachers or something...! They might revise your score if you did!"

I'm not so sure...

Although Otoleanna Academy had a liberal atmosphere, tests were handled strictly. She couldn't imagine a score that had been posted on the bulletin board being revised. But something else bothered her more. She rested her hand gently on Kira's shoulder and said, as calmly as possible, "I don't know about that—but, Kira, did someone make you do it?"

"What?"

"If something is still bothering you, you can tell me."

She doesn't seem like the type to do something so underhanded.

Plus, despite her terror, she didn't appear to have anything against Brigitte. Brigitte's guess was that Kira had been used by someone who did hate Brigitte. In which case, Brigitte was part of the reason this happened. And she couldn't very well leave such a timid girl to her own devices.

At the very least, I have to make sure this person doesn't use Kira again...

Kira twined her hands together, as if she was trying to pretend she didn't know.

"You're very kind, Miss Brigitte."

"Huh?"

"I mean, something bad happened to you because of me...but you're still worried about me."

"But..."

"And then you came to my rescue when I was in trouble in the woods...just like a knight in shining armor!"

"But—but..."

Kira went on tearfully, but Brigitte could no longer hear her.

Me, 'kind?' No one has ever called me that before...!

She felt as if her face was on fire from bashfulness. Kind, really? Not Brigitte!

She had completely forgotten that Nival had said the same thing to her two weeks earlier. She had assumed he was just delusional.

She coughed and glanced at Kira. "You really think I'm kind?"

"You are kind! As kind and beautiful as a goddess. You have a very loving heart!"

"That's going a bit far."

"No, it's true!!" she shouted so loudly, Brigitte wondered if her quiet voice earlier was just an act. Kira's zeal was getting overwhelming.

"Anyway," Brigitte said, going back to their earlier conversation. "Are you sure everything is all right with the person who made you do it?"

"It's fine. I'll convince her." Her pretty black eyes peered out from between her black bangs. "I'll tell her that we can apologize to you together. So please...can you just wait a little longer?"

Brigitte looked at her in surprise...then smiled.

She's not timid at all!

She had her own ideas. Brigitte didn't need to worry so much about it.

"...All right, I'll wait."

"Thank you! I promise I won't ever do anything like that again! I swear my loyalty to you for life! Please don't abandon me!"

"What? Of course I w-won't. I would never abandon you."

"Oh, Miss Brigitte...!"

Kira's eyes grew moist with emotion.

At the same moment, Brigitte thought she heard a deep voice calling her name from far away.

Am I hearing things, or was that the voice of a certain class president?

From the corner of her eye, she saw the brownie jumping for joy as it discovered the magic stone she had buried.

The rain finally lifted around evening. That was enough for Brigitte to breathe more easily.

I've always hated rainy days...

The memory of that awful day came back to her so vividly. Somehow, though, she managed to push down the indelible afterimages that still tormented her and look out at their surroundings.

The sky was already dark, and she could hardly see into the forest. Searching for magic stones in an unfamiliar environment could be dangerous. She glanced back at Kira. She didn't see the brownie in the cave anymore. Appearing in the human world consumed an enormous amount of magical energy. Brigitte guessed it had returned to the spirit world to recover its strength. Maybe that was why Kira looked slightly tired herself... But more likely, she was worn down from the test. She hadn't said much for a while.

"Should we camp here for the night?" Brigitte asked.

"Y-yes, I suppose. We should probably make a fire, don't you think?"

Brigitte shook her head. "...I don't think we need one. We have food and water." Kira nodded, and Brigitte remembered something she'd wanted to tell her. As she took her rations out of her knapsack, she said casually, "By the way, Kira, I think you'd look good with your bangs pulled back."

"Huh?"

"Your eyes are quite pretty," she said candidly.

"...!" Kira gasped. "...You really think so?"

"Yes—at least in my opinion."

"Thank you, Miss Brigitte."

There was something stiff about her response. Brigitte wondered if she'd said something wrong. But when she looked up, something else caught her attention.

A light was flickering at the mouth of the cave.

The long shadow that covered Brigitte and Kira wavered. When Brigitte turned around in surprise, her breath stopped.

Miss Selmin...?

Lisa was standing in the entrance, holding a torch. She must have gotten drenched in the rain, because water was dripping from her hair and clothes. Brigitte couldn't see the expression on her downturned face, but something was clearly different from usual.

"Lisa...?" Kira called uneasily.

Brigitte noticed that Lisa's mouth was moving.

"It's all your fault... Yes, you..." She was mumbling something, but the echoes in the narrow cave made it hard to hear clearly.

"...Kira, I'll distract her. Will you find someone and ask them to come here?"

"What? B-but..."

"Something seems wrong. I would be very grateful if you could go for help."

Kira nodded hesitantly. Brigitte called to Lisa, keeping her voice calm to avoid agitating her.

"Miss Selmin, do you need something?"

"!"

Her reaction was dramatic.

"Brigitte...Brigitte Meidell!!"

Brigitte and Kira froze at Lisa's terrible expression. Her bloodshot eyes were bulging, and her lips were bleeding from being chewed. Her normally neat hair was plastered to her forehead and cheeks.

What in the world happened...?

Brigitte had felt Lisa's animosity many times, but she had never feared for her life before. Brigitte was stunned, but she pushed Kira's back gently forward. Kira jumped, then slipped past Lisa.

"...Be careful, Miss Brigitte!" she called before vanishing into the darkness. Left alone, Brigitte tried to keep her face blank as she turned to Lisa, but—

"...Why?" Lisa muttered, like she was talking to herself.

Brigitte frowned.

"Why are Sir Nival and even Kira suddenly your slaves?"

Brigitte wasn't sure how to answer. "They're not my slaves," she said. "Nival and Kira are my friends."

At least I think they are...

Lisa couldn't have heard the anxious voice in her mind, but she brandished her torch and screamed, "The Red Fairy will never have *friends!*"

Brigitte stumbled backward. Lisa's shadow wavered ominously, like a giant about to swallow her up.

"...Oh, I see," Lisa growled.

Goose bumps rose all over Brigitte's body.

"You're scared of fire, aren't you, Brigitte?"

"...!"

She stiffened, and Lisa seemed to recognize her nervous fear.

"It does make sense. Your own father burned your hand, after all!" She cackled. "Ah-ha-ha, how funny. Poor Brigitte! You really are a miserable, shameful person!"

Before she knew what she was doing, her right hand was pressing her gloved left hand protectively. Although she was drenched with cold sweat, she smiled defiantly.

"...Yes, you're right, Miss Selmin."

"...What?"

Lisa must not have expected her to accept these insults, and she narrowed her eyes threateningly.

Brigitte looked straight at her and smiled again. She was afraid her voice would waver or tears would spill from her eyes, but she refused to be defeated by someone who used words like knives to mock people.

I can't let her win...

"Imagine, the daughter of the Fire Clan being afraid of fire! I agree, it's laughable. So laugh as much as you please," she said.

"...What, are you bluffing?"

"No, I'm telling you the truth. Like you said—it's laughable, isn't it?" she declared. "So go on and laugh. I don't care."

Lisa looked taken aback, but the violent hatred in her eyes only intensified.

"Oh, ha-ha, I just had a lovely idea..."

There was a twisted elation growing in the ugly smile on her face. She raised her torch like a sword.

"Red Fairy, how would you like to burn your hand one more time with this flame?"

She heard the footsteps behind her and saw the flickering flame. Brigitte was running through the forest, glancing over her shoulder again and again.

"Huff..."

Everything had gone well until she was out of the cave. But Lisa was surprisingly fast, and the distance between them wasn't growing.

—No, the truth was, Brigitte's body wasn't moving how she wanted it to. That was why she couldn't get away from Lisa.

Those flames...

All the cottage servants knew Brigitte's past and kept her away from fire. And she herself never went near places where it was used, like the kitchen or the incinerator. The same was true at school. She took great care not to witness fire spirits performing magic when she saw them on the street or at school.

That was why now—

The flames chasing her looked like enormous waves. Sometimes they reached out like her father's arm and tried to consume her.

"...!"

She clenched her jaw and ran desperately forward. Each time her feet hit the damp ground, mud splattered around them. Her strength was draining away. But she couldn't stop because she didn't know what Lisa would do to her if she did.

She had underestimated Lisa, however. Maybe she was annoyed at not being able to catch up. Whatever the reason, she threw her torch—and it came flying toward Brigitte's head.

"No—"

Brigitte couldn't move. She could only stare at the flames raging madly as they fell toward her. She couldn't breathe, couldn't run.

Crash!!

But a second later, the torch was repelled backward and fell at Lisa's feet.

Only then did Brigitte remember. Though her vision was clouded by sweat dripping into her eyes, his handsome face seemed to glow before her.

Yuri...

Her hair was fastened at the back of her head by the ornament he'd given her. It was a magic item of the finest quality, said to repel any type of magic one time. Of the nine jewels on the ornament, the red one would have lost its glow. It had repelled Lisa's attack, serving its purpose.

Did that mean he had foreseen something like this happening—and given her the ornament for that reason?

It's like Yuri protected me...

But even as a faint wave of relief and courage washed over her, she realized something else. The fire of Lisa's torch had not been lit by her but rather bestowed by fire magic.

That was odd.

I'm sure the type of magic Lisa uses is—

"—How is this possible?!"

Her train of thought was cut off by Lisa's scream slicing through the blackness.

"Y-you're contracted with a no-name, aren't you...?! You shouldn't have that kind of power!!"

She seemed to be assuming that Brigitte's contracted spirit had repulsed her attack. Brigitte was going to say something—but then pressed her lips shut.

If I tell her the truth—that a magic item protected me—she'll attack me again...

Although attacks on other students during the magic-stone hunt were forbidden, Lisa had broken the rule openly. And the torch at her feet was still burning weakly. It would be foolish to give away her secret right now.

But as she stood there silently, fury swelled inside Lisa.

"Why?! You're a stupid, useless dunce, and everyone hates you! So how did you do that?! Tell me!!"

"Miss Selmin..."

"Shut up!"

She grabbed the fallen torch. Brigitte braced herself, but Lisa did not brandish it at her. Instead, she carelessly touched it to her own right arm.

"What are you doing?!"

Brigitte had no time to stop her. The terrifying sound of sizzling skin was all she could hear.

"Ahhhh!"

"…!"

As Brigitte watched, Lisa screamed in agony. But she did not stop until she was severely burned, and then the torch fell from her hand.

"Ah, ah-ha-ha. It's so hot…"

As she writhed in pain, large tears splashed from her eyes, and snot poured from her nose. When Brigitte saw her face, she sank to the ground.

"It hurts! You're burning me! Please stop!"

"Please, please! Please, Father, forgive me…!"

The distant memory sprang back to life. A cold sweat froze her body. The image of her own young self crying and screaming layered on top of Lisa as she cried and cackled.

"What are you doing?"

At that moment, several students and Marjory Naha came running toward them. Brigitte had assumed that Ms. Naha and her many korpukkur helpers were overseeing the test, and it seemed her guess had been right.

Behind her were Kira, Nival, and…Yuri. Kira must have asked them to help as Brigitte had requested. She was panting and looking worriedly at Brigitte. But Brigitte said nothing.

Ms. Naha looked back and forth between Lisa and Brigitte, who was sitting dazed in the muddy road.

"What is going on here? Brigitte? Lisa?" she asked, her expression confused but stern.

©Yomi Sarachi

What do I do? I can't talk.

She had plenty to say in her own defense, but her mouth refused to open. She was in shock.

"...Brigitte?"

Kira must have filled in Ms. Naha because she was watching her new friend with concern. But Lisa interrupted.

"Ms. Naha?"

"Do you have something to say, Lisa?"

Lisa nodded, her face terrifyingly blank. She stuck out her right arm.

"Brigitte Meidell burned me."

As Ms. Naha ran toward her, the forest went silent...and then immediately filled with gossip.

CHAPTER 8

People Who Believe in Me

"Miss Meidell burned Miss Selmin's arm?"

"Imagine doing something so violent in the middle of a test!"

"But I thought the Red Fairy had turned over a new leaf…"

The comments were flying so fast, Brigitte thought the trees might start swaying. Lisa was shaking as Ms. Naha held her. But Brigitte could see the smile on her lips.

"Hush, hush, everyone," Ms. Naha said for the tenth time, but the students ignored her.

The students scattered through the woods must have heard the fuss, because they were arriving in a steady stream. And most were staring rudely at Brigitte. Sitting in the muddy road, she watched them detachedly.

…Just like always.

She had tried to change starting on the day Joseph ended their engagement.

From an arrogant person to a slightly down-to-earth one.

From ugly clothes to ones she liked a little more.

She had faced her problems head-on. She'd wanted to peel off her heavy makeup and try smiling one day.

Even here at the magic-stone hunt, I was trying so hard!
Despite all that, people were talking about her again. She was too overwhelmed by that reality to speak or stand up.

In the end, I—

"Brigitte."

Suddenly, she heard a voice right next to her. She looked fearfully up...and was shocked to see someone she'd assumed had already left.

"Sir Yuri..."

There was tension on his face instead of his usual cool detachment.

"Brigitte, don't look at the ground."

His voice was distinctly lower than usual.

She wondered if he was angry with her for spoiling their competition. She stared harder at the ground, growing increasingly frightened. She was used to other people looking down on her. But Yuri—if Yuri did the same, well... Even the thought was enough to make her feel like she was choking.

Don't cry...

She sniffled. Yuri shook her shoulder with a hint of frustration.

"Brigitte, can you hear me?"

"..."

"You didn't do it, did you? Then hold your head high!"

Huh?

She couldn't believe her ears. When she jerked her face up, he was looking straight at her. His eyes glowed with conviction and not a hint of dishonesty.

"I never doubted you, and neither did those two."

Brigitte looked behind him. "Those two?"

"You still don't remember our names, do you, Yuri...?"

There was a grumpy Nival and a despondent Kira.

Oh...

She finally understood.

She hadn't seen anything in the darkness.

She had assumed that everyone hated her again. But when she finally looked around, she saw that most of her classmates were watching her anxiously. They were concerned for her, as if that was the natural response to all this. As for Yuri, he was smiling so faintly, she wasn't sure if she was imagining it. That slightly ironic smile was so like him.

"Do you understand now? I'm saying we believe you."

"...!"

The world blurred, and Brigitte scrubbed her eyes. This was no time to cry. She had something important to do.

"Can you stand?"

"Yes, I'm fine."

Rejecting the arm he offered, she stood up slowly. She tottered slightly, but she felt much stronger than she had a few minutes ago.

Calm down. Breathe in, breathe out. You're fine...

"Ms. Naha?"

She managed to keep her voice from shaking. Ms. Naha looked rather nonplussed with Lisa clinging to her. She gazed at Brigitte.

"Ms. Naha, I did not hurt Miss Selmin," she said confidently. Another buzz ran through the gathered students.

Kira stepped forward. "I can testify to what I saw. Li...Miss Lisa suddenly appeared with a torch at the cave where Miss Brigitte and I were resting. Miss Brigitte told me to run for help, since something seemed very wrong!"

Kira must have been terrified to stand up in front of so many people, because her legs were shaking, and her voice broke...but for Brigitte's sake, she stayed where she was.

Lisa stared at the two of them hatefully.

"Don't let them fool you! They're liars!" she screamed. "Ms. Naha, Brigitte has been harassing me because she's jealous of my relationship with Prince Joseph! She's trying to frame me again!"

The contradictory stories inspired another rising wave of hubbub, and Ms. Naha seemed unsure what to do. As a teacher, she could not casually take one side or the other.

If there was only some proof...

Brigitte racked her brain. She thought about showing her the hair ornament that had partially broken after being used...but that wouldn't be decisive. Plus, although Brigitte was contracted with a tiny spirit whose type of magic she didn't even know, she belonged to the Fire Clan. If someone accused her of breaking the hair ornament herself, she'd have no response.

Just then, as if to ease the deadlock, a gentle voice rang out overhead.

"If you please, I can solve this problem," the familiar female voice said. Brigitte looked up in surprise.

The undine?

Yuri's contracted spirit came floating down delicately from midair.

"Is it real...?!"

"Wow, what a beautiful spirit..."

Excitement ran through the crowd at the sudden appearance of such a lovely first-class spirit. Opportunities to glimpse the spirits that stood at the pinnacle of their countless peers were extremely rare.

Yuri, however, sighed and grimaced. "I was wondering where you went..."

"My apologies, master. This brook is very pleasant."

She giggled seductively. Even in the dark, Brigitte could see several students blush.

That reminds me...

The forest surrounded the academy, and a brook ran alongside its edge. She had seen Yuri letting his undine play in that stream before, and now she realized the undine had probably been doing exactly as she pleased.

"...Undine, did you appear just now for the reason I think?"

"Indeed. How like you to understand so quickly, master." Then in a casual but far-reaching voice, she said, "Have those of you gathered here heard of the undines' reflecting pool?"

Brigitte knew instantly what she meant.

It can't be...

Reflecting pools were a special skill of undines. Once they saw something, they had the power to re-create it on the water's surface. A tragic short story called "Undine's Reflecting Pool" told of an undine who used this skill to reveal her human husband's unfaithfulness, only to be killed in retaliation. The story was so famous, everyone in the crowd likely knew it.

As the meaning of the spirit's words sank in, a murmur spread among the students. The undine gazed calmly over the crowd. She smiled, pressing her palms to her cheeks. To Brigitte, it was the smile of a goddess, but to Lisa, who had turned a ghostly white, it would have been the smile of a demon.

"I saw that girl press the torch to her own arm," the undine said, giggling. "Shall I reflect it in my pool?"

A painful silence fell over the woods. The students must have understood everything in an instant. They saw how agitated Lisa was. And in direct contrast, they saw Brigitte sighing in relief at her unforeseen good fortune. Who was speaking the truth and who was lying?

It was Ms. Naha who broke the silence.

"Thank you, undine. I am grateful for your cooperation," she said, her stern tone a moment earlier replaced by her usual gentleness.

"There's no need to thank me. I simply couldn't stand by and watch a girl in trouble."

She glanced gracefully at Brigitte and winked. Brigitte smiled back awkwardly.

"For the sake of formality, I would like to look at the reflecting pool with the other teachers. Brigitte, is that all right with you?" Ms. Naha asked.

"Yes, of course."

"Lisa, no objections?"

"Um...uh...we don't need to look at it!" Lisa was frantic, perhaps realizing the situation had taken a turn.

"Of course we do. If a reflecting pool can show us the truth, won't it prove your innocence?"

"B-but...the undine is Sir Yuri's contracted spirit! Brigitte's been currying favor with Sir Yuri. Please don't trust the reflecting pool!"

"...Lisa."

Lisa flinched.

"You have called another student a liar in public. Do you understand what that means?"

"...!!"

The students who were watching whispered mercilessly among themselves as they stared at the profoundly miserable Lisa. Brigitte didn't enjoy witnessing this, but at least Ms. Naha seemed to be giving Lisa basic consideration.

"Students, the test is temporarily suspended. Everyone will return to the academy dorms for the night. Boarding students, please use your own rooms. Everyone else, the annex is open, so you may sleep there. My spirits will notify any students who have not yet gathered here," Ms. Naha announced briskly before dispatching her korpukkurs. Then she began walking, one hand on the shoulder of the listless, downcast Lisa.

Several students followed her, looking confused. The students in Brigitte's class tried to run over to her, but Nival held them back.

"Come on, everyone, let's go to the dorms. The road is dark, so those of you who can use light magic, please make some lanterns," he said, assuming his role as the class president. Just before the class set off together, he looked back and pointed sharply at Yuri, his eyes wide.

"You owe me—you got that, Yuri?"

"...Then don't make me go into debt in the first place."

"Nice try! ...I'm counting on you, dammit!" he shouted as he disappeared into the darkness.

Kira walked up to Brigitte, her eyes darting around nervously. "Miss Brigitte, I—"

"It's all right. I'll walk her back to school," Yuri interrupted.

"...Oh. I'll just run to the cave and get the bags we left there, then!"

Yuri watched her run anxiously off before looking up.

"It's not often that you help someone like that," he said.

"I could say the same about you, master," his undine replied, smiling as she flipped in midair to wave her tail. "Good-bye for now. I'll leave the Red Fairy to you."

With that, the undine melted into the air. The woods were so silent Brigitte almost wondered if she had imagined the uproar earlier.

Yuri was watching her. "Brigitte."

"..."

"Brigitte?"

His voice was unbelievably kind. Although she had been unable to speak until then, her energy suddenly drained away, and she blurted out, "...I was so scared."

He did not laugh. Instead, he simply nodded and said, "Ah." All the feelings she'd been holding back began to pour out.

"I couldn't stand it, not again— It was so painful; it hurt so badly..."

"...I know."

Something was stroking her head gently. It took her a few seconds to realize it was the palm of his hand.

"You were so strong...Brigitte."

"..."

Tears sprang to her eyes. She couldn't be strong any longer. She threw her arms around his chest.

"Whoa!"

She pretended not to hear his obviously reluctant yelp. Her eyes were hot behind her tightly closed eyelids. Tears kept falling until she wondered if they would melt her cheeks right off. A pitiful wheezing sound escaped her throat. She was like a little child letting their most miserable self be seen.

Yuri didn't seem to know how to respond. "Why are you crying?"

Even his voice wavered with confusion.

"Because you're saying things that make me cry."

She knew it wasn't fair to blame him. But if she didn't say something, she didn't think she would be able to keep breathing.

"...I see. Then cry as much as you want; it's my fault."

Even his exasperated nod was unbearably kind. So she went on sobbing convulsively, whimpering every now and then.

©Yomi Sarachi

After a few minutes, once she had calmed down slightly, she abruptly came to her senses.

Wh-what in the world am I doing...?!

No matter how upset she was, there were standards for proper behavior. The daughters of noblemen weren't supposed to cry themselves into delirium with no control over their emotions. She stopped crying from shock, only to realize something mortifying.

"I'm s-s-sorry; I got snot on you...!"

But when she tried to pull away, he pulled her closer, and his arm softly trapped her. It was surprisingly warm for someone called the Frozen Blade. At the mercy of that warmth she had longed for, she whispered, "Thank you...Sir Yuri."

"...It's nothing."

"It's nothing, master? I believe *I* was the one who rescued the charming fairy from a tight spot?"

Brigitte leaped away from Yuri at the sound of the undine's voice. She had been able to lean on Yuri when she thought no one was watching—but if a witness was present, that was a different story.

Was she watching this whole time?!

She was so unsettled that she didn't notice Yuri grumpily cross his outstretched arms.

"I'll load you up with magic water stones," he said.

"Water stones? That's all? How about some holy water, too?"

Yuri sighed and gave the tiniest nod.

As Brigitte listened to them, something struck her as odd.

His darling Miss Selmin was in all that trouble, and yet...

Joseph hadn't once shown his face.

The following week, a noisy crowd of second-year students stood in front of the bulletin board, checking their test results.

"Wow, Miss Brigitte's done it again...!"

"She's so amazing!"

The results of the pre-summer-vacation magic-stone hunt had been posted. Yuri was in the top place, and Brigitte was in second. Meanwhile, Nival and Kira looked up at their names excitedly. Their classmates soon joined them, surrounding Brigitte in a celebratory crowd.

But Brigitte herself was unable to hide her shock, even as she fanned herself and blustered, "Ah-ha-ha, it is what it is."

...He won!!

The hunt had never been rescheduled after it was suspended due to the incident with Lisa, so the results were based solely on the first day of magic-stone collecting.

Yuri had eight magic stones.

Brigitte had seven.

Everyone else had four, three, or less. That was why Brigitte was getting so much attention despite not being in first place. But all she could see was his name.

If I'd just gotten a few more...!

She was confident that if she'd been able to hunt freely on the second day, she'd have gotten more than on the first. She'd already identified a few spots where she was certain she could have found many spirits.

It's so maddening...!

Secretly shaking with frustration, she turned to Kira and whispered, "Are you sure you didn't mind?"

"What?"

"The magic stone. You gave me one, remember?"

On the night of the magic-stone hunt, Yuri had walked her to the dorms. She'd never been inside before, but when she came in, feeling flustered, Kira handed her her knapsack and a magic stone. Kira said she had found two of them in the cave where they sheltered. A spirit must have hidden them away from people or other spirits and then forgotten about them. Brigitte had refused at first, saying Kira should keep them both, since she'd found them, but Kira insisted, so in the end, Brigitte had ended up with her seventh stone. But it meant she'd stolen a point from Kira.

"I wanted you to have it," Kira mumbled shyly. "I...thought it was like something from a story."

Brigitte nodded. Now it made sense.

"You mean like the scene in *The Wind Laughs*, where Professor Lien and the sylphide break a magic stone in half and each take one piece as a talisman?"

"Yes, exactly!" Kira answered excitedly, pressing her palms to her flushed cheeks.

"I wanted our relationship to be like the one between Lien Baluanuki and the sylphide—"

"What are you talking about? Don't you know all the magic stones from the hunt got collected?" interrupted Nival, who had been listening in.

Kira pouted. Then, brightening, she pushed up her long bangs. Her eyes, as black as the night sky, appeared.

"Miss Brigitte told me my eyes are pretty," she said.

She's so cute!

Maybe she meant to threaten Nival by staring at him...but seeing her whole face for the first time, Brigitte found her lovely. She had big moist eyes and small pink lips. She was like an adorable little animal.

A buzz went through the other students who were watching. Brigitte guessed they were startled by the sudden realization that their classmate was beautiful. She understood how they felt. But Nival stepped forward and glared mercilessly at Kira.

"Is that so? Well, one time, Miss Brigitte told me I was amazing because I climbed the stairs two at a time!"

"Miss Brigitte gave my b-brownie a magic stone."

"Oh yeah? I ate lunch outside with Miss Brigitte and my ariel once!"

"I bet that's only because Miss Brigitte wanted to talk to her!"

While the two of them were caught up in this incomprehensible argument, Brigitte snuck silently away.

After school, Brigitte tucked her books in her bag and headed straight to the library. She took the path that led back to the garden...and as the gazebo came into view for what felt like the first time in ages, she caught a glimpse of silky blue-black hair. He must have been reading a book, because the round back of his head was tilted adorably downward.

"Yu—"

She was about to call his name, but then she stopped. The memory of revealing so much of her raw emotions to him was still fresh...and mortifying. He probably thought it was trivial. She wanted to act like nothing had happened, but that was impossible.

He's always seeing my weak side...

She secretly wished she had a few of *his* weak points in her back pocket. Apparently sensing her evil intentions, however, he looked over his shoulder.

"What are you doing standing there?" he asked.

"Nothing!" she answered, flustered, and sat down across from him.

He shut his book, and they stared silently at each other. That was enough to make her heart pound.

"The hair ornament...," she began.

He raised his eyebrows. Too embarrassed to look him in the eye, she lowered her gaze.

"Thank you. Did you guess from the start that something like that would happen…?"

"…Who knows? People dislike you about as much as they dislike me."

Brigitte remembered saying something similar to him once. He smiled slightly, his elbow propped on the table and his chin in his hand. This was nothing like his usual cold, blank expression; it set her heart racing.

To cover it up, she said, "And the reflecting pool…"

"I didn't have anything to do with that," he answered.

The undine's reflecting pool had saved her. Ms. Naha and the other teachers had said that when they looked in, they saw the reflection of Lisa pressing the torch to her own arm, clear as day. She was suspended for a week—but although the week was over, she still hadn't left her dorm room.

Lisa's room was next to Kira's, and Kira said she visited every day, but so far Lisa hadn't said a word. Brigitte knew she ought to talk to Lisa herself, but she was hesitant to make her feel any more harassed. Also, Kira and Lisa had been childhood friends, since their families ruled over neighboring domains. Kira had told Brigitte to leave everything in her hands, and she was.

"Anyway, about the competition," Yuri said. Brigitte pressed her lips together. "According to the results on the bulletin board, I win."

She hadn't seen him there at lunch when the results were posted, but evidently, he'd checked at some point.

"…Yes. Congratulations."

She'd expected him to act indifferent, but this time, his reaction was slightly unusual. He sighed as if something was bothering him.

"…Thanks, but the truth is, I got only two of them myself."

Did that mean his contracted spirits collected the other six?

If that was the case, it still boiled down to his own ability. No matter how reluctant he was, she intended to accept his victory.

A loss is a loss. I'm not going to try to weasel out of this!

"…The loser has to do whatever the winner says, right?" His citrine eyes narrowed provocatively, fixed solely on her. "Will you come to my house?"

I'm hearing things.

That was her immediate thought.

Ugh, I must be awfully tired.

"I'm sorry, Sir Yuri. I didn't hear you."

"I said, will you come to my house?"

Strange. Her ears were still acting up. She asked him again, puzzled.

"What?"

"Will you come to my house?"

"What?"

"…Will you come to my house?"

"What?"

"Will you… Oh, forget it, if you hate the idea that much."

He looked away. She finally realized he was genuinely asking her to come visit.

"N-no, that's not it! I just thought I misheard you!"

Although she frantically tried to explain, he blanched slightly, as if he had just realized the implications of what he'd said.

Going to his house would have been perfectly normal if they were dating or engaged. But right now, he'd basically ordered a girl who'd lost a competition with him to do so. That changed the meaning a little—a lot, really.

I can't let myself imagine such improper things!

She shook her head to chase the images away.

Anyhow, this was Yuri Aurealis, a member of the Water Clan. She couldn't imagine him asking her over for risqué reasons. He was hardly lacking for willing female companionship. Why in the world would he invite someone as unpopular as her over when plenty of other attractive girls were interested?

"...I understand why you don't want to, but right now, I can't tell you the reason I'm asking you to come."

Of c-course. I know there's some reason—an important one!

Brigitte nodded, pretending to be calm while hiding her mouth with her fan.

"...I'll g-go."

"Ah. I'm glad."

"..."

"..."

An awkward silence descended. Brigitte stood up stiffly, afraid that if she stayed, she would say something she regretted.

"You're going home?"

"Um, yes, I-I'll go now."

I can't even speak clearly!

As she took an unsteady step, he said, "By the way."

She blinked, wondering what he would say. He fixed his piercing gaze on her.

"Congratulations on winning second place, Brigitte."

"—Th-thank you."

She walked out of the gazebo. As she hurried away, she couldn't help smiling and, finally, laughing a little. She pressed her palms against her disobedient cheeks.

She knew it was childish, but she was happy he'd complimented her. She'd come in second, behind him—but it still mattered that he recognized the accomplishment.

Being with him is always fun.

He was so rude with his words, but he was kind with his actions. When she thought about their conversations afterward, sometimes she wanted to cover her face or squirm in embarrassment, but their time together was the most special thing in her life.

…This must be what people meant by happiness.

Still, she was so flustered, she didn't know what to do with herself.

If I'm going to his house, I'd better bring some kind of present… Maybe I'll ask Sienna for advice.

She'd been too shaken until now to consider the fact that she was going to the residence of the famous Water Clan, the House of Aurealis. If she was lucky, she might see some more water or ice spirits. Her heart leaped at the thought.

If nobody was around, she would have skipped all the way to the carriage stop.

But when she got there, she noticed a tall figure standing on the paving stones, evidently waiting for her.

Why…?

She stopped and stared in disbelief. The person sensed her and turned slowly around—his hair and eyes were golden.

It was the Third Prince of the Kingdom of Field—Brigitte's former fiancé.

"…Prince…Joseph?"

They stared at each other at close range for the first time in a month. Brigitte couldn't move.

The same lips that had coldly broken off their engagement slowly began to move, forming a soft arc.

"Let's get engaged again. Will you make a fresh start with me, Brigitte?"

A Place to Come Home to

On that day, Sienna saw Brigitte off to school before heading into the capital to do some shopping. While her mistress was at the academy of magic, Sienna had things to do. Selecting makeup, clothes, shoes, accessories, and other small items was an important part of her job as a waiting maid.

Today, she was visiting her favorite stores to buy clothes that would suit Brigitte. For a while, following the orders of her fiancé, Prince Joseph, Brigitte had worn only dramatic makeup and pink dresses. But now that Brigitte was free from what Sienna thought of as Joseph's spell, Sienna was dying to turn her adorable mistress into the best-dressed girl around.

As she adjusted a parcel containing a new outfit in her arms, she wished Brigitte had been able to come with her. Of course, she knew her mistress's measurements and favorite colors and styles by heart. But it was hard to imagine exactly how everything would work with her coloring or how things would feel when she had it on. And since Sienna was petite with orange hair while Brigitte was tall with bright red hair, there was no way Sienna could try things on for her.

...Of course, that was all just an excuse. The truth was, she simply wanted to go out with Brigitte.

Snap out of it! You can't keep her all to yourself!

To get herself back in line, she tugged at her cheeks. But even as she did, she couldn't help wondering what Brigitte was doing right then.

Although she had seemed depressed for a few days after the prince ended their engagement, lately she was acting quite cheerful. Sienna guessed that was thanks to the friends she'd made at school, like Yuri, Nival, and Kira. She had found a new place for herself at the academy. Although Sienna was happy for her, she felt a little sad that she hadn't been able to help her mistress more.

I made so many mistakes right from the start...

She thought guiltily back on the bitter past.

There weren't many servants at the Meidell cottage. Most had been transferred there from the main residence by the Earl of Meidell because he said they were bad at their jobs.

Sienna was among them.

At first, she had been placed in the main house as a waiting maid in training, but after being accused of being unfriendly and not getting along with the other servants, she was sent to the newly built cottage.

She had been born into a merchant family distantly related to the Meidells—although her family wasn't very well-off. As the youngest of eight children, she had been in service to the Meidells at the age of seven so her parents would have one less mouth to feed.

Soon after that, her whole family moved. They did not tell her where they went. She realized then that they had abandoned her. She was not an expressive child, and even in her own family, she had been the odd one out. Her parents must have been overjoyed to not only pawn her off on the Meidells but even receive moving money in return.

She decided then to make her own way in the world. She thought selfishly that if she rose to a position as waiting maid in the noted Fire Clan, she might make a good match in the future.

But just months after beginning her training, Sienna was transferred to the cottage. Most of the other transferred servants were sympathetic with Brigitte and carried out their duties gallantly— but not Sienna. She turned her anger at her own situation against the little girl.

Crash! The glass shattered noisily.

"I'm s-sorry."

How many times had she heard those words already that day?

Sienna sighed with frustration. Brigitte's shoulders shook in fear, which only irritated Sienna more. Everyone said her young mistress had been an innocent child before the move. She loved spirits and spent her days poring over books and stories about them or escaping the mansion to search for fairies. Sienna had seen the servants chasing desperately after her many times. But right now, she was staring at the floor, her fiery red hair hanging over her face. Her bandaged left hand was shaking. Shards of glass were scattered beneath a chair along with the hand mirror she must have dropped.

"You do not need to apologize. I'll clean it up. Will you please move aside?" Sienna snapped.

"…Yes…," Brigitte said sadly as she walked obediently away.

Sienna fetched a broom from the closet and briskly swept up the glass. She never cut corners on her work, no matter how trivial the task. Whether it was cleaning, laundry, or errands that needed doing, she always took the lead.

So why did I get stuck taking care of this girl?

She'd been moved from the enormous, beautiful main house to this cottage built to imprison a little girl. To make matters worse, the cottage had certain peculiarities.

First, it was hidden away behind the main house, largely out of view of the people there. Everyone whispered that the earl truly must not want to lay eyes on his only daughter.

Second, there was no means of heating the cottage. The most conspicuous example was the lack of fireplaces. There wasn't a single one in the whole place. This was because, several weeks earlier, Brigitte's father had burned her hand in the hearth after she failed to contract with a desirable spirit. The kitchen and the incinerator, too, functioned with as little fire as possible, and the servants always checked to make sure Brigitte wasn't nearby when they used them.

These oddities struck Sienna as foolish. It was all well and good now, in June, but how were they supposed to get through the colder months? Winters in the capital were frigid. Temperatures dipped below freezing some nights. Her irritation grew more and more.

One day, when Brigitte came to her yet again to apologize, Sienna blurted out, "Instead of apologizing all the time, I wish you'd send me back to the main house."

She clapped her hand over her mouth. She knew she'd made a mistake. Brigitte was the one who'd been chased out of the main house. And now she was asking that same girl to return her there?

"I didn't mean—," she began. But Brigitte's response surprised her.

"...I know. I'm sorry. I don't know what he'll say, but I will ask my father," she mumbled, her head still lowered.

Sienna looked down coldly at the girl.

If you can't promise me anything, then just say that.

Brigitte must be trying to curry favor by getting her hopes up. She couldn't have meant what she said. In a few days, she'd probably say, "*Sorry, he said no,*" or just pretend to forget all about it. So Sienna decided to forget about it, too. Because of that, she also forgot to apologize for what she'd said.

The next day, when Sienna went outside to sweep the stoop, she heard a child's pleading voice some distance away.

"Please, I'm begging you."

Is that the mistress?

The voice seemed to be coming from the main house. Brigitte must have slipped out of the cottage to beg for a doll or something. After making sure no one was nearby, Sienna snuck to a spot where she could see the back door of the main house. Normally she wasn't allowed there, but she was too curious to resist.

What she saw caught her completely by surprise.

Brigitte, her back to Sienna, was bowing doggedly to the main-house butler.

"You can put me in a closet all by myself. Please just let Sienna and everyone else go back to the house. Please."

The butler looked like he didn't know how to react to the desperate pleas of his master's daughter. When the earl had thrust her hand into the fire, the aged butler had immediately tried to stop him. Sienna had seen with her own eyes his swollen cheek after the master punched him—although the wound was fully healed now thanks to the priest's magic.

"Miss…I understand your feelings, but please calm down. If the master sees you…"

"If he did, could I talk to him? I only want to ask Father to take Sienna back."

"Miss…"

Even from a distance, Sienna could see that Brigitte was shaking. Her shaking increased when she said the word *Father.* Of course it did. Only weeks before, he had burned her hand. She was probably still terrified and worried out of her mind. Nevertheless, she was begging on Sienna's behalf.

"Miss!"

Unable to stay silent any longer, Sienna shot forward. Brigitte looked back in surprise. Suddenly, her little body tottered sideways. Sienna rushed to catch her. Her skin was sweltering.

"She has a fever...," the butler said, easily lifting her panting, limp body from Sienna's arms. After glancing around, he walked swiftly toward the cottage. Flustered, Sienna followed.

"It's an aftereffect of her wound. Burns can cause severe fever and delirium," he explained over his shoulder.

I had no idea...

Brigitte had always apologized to Sienna with her head hanging. Afterward, she would retreat alone to her room. She must have cried there. Overtaken by fever, she must have suffered alone.

I didn't know anything.

Tears blurred Sienna's eyes. She hadn't cried once when her parents abandoned her or when the head maid scolded her. But even after the butler carried Brigitte to her room and laid her on her big bed, Sienna continued to cry so hard, she couldn't speak. The old butler leaned over and looked her in the eye.

"Sienna. I have to leave now."

He probably didn't want to go. She could hear the distress in his voice and see it on his face.

"I need you to prepare clean linens and ice water for the young miss. There is cream for her left hand on the shelf. She knows how to use it."

"..."

"You are her attendant now. Can you do those things?"

"Yes…yes," Sienna said, wiping her tears. The butler nodded with relief.

By the time she got back to the room with linens and ice water, the butler was gone. Brigitte gazed vacantly at Sienna from the bed. Sienna walked nervously up to her. She managed to set the heavy pail of ice water next to the bed. Plunging her hands into the cold water, she wet a towel and wrung it out. First she placed the towel on Brigitte's forehead, and Brigitte's face relaxed slightly at the cool touch. She was so hot that the towel would probably need to be changed soon. Sienna wanted to wipe down her sweat-slick body, too, but there was something more important to do first.

"Miss, may I remove your bandage?"

The girl didn't answer. Taking this as a tacit yes, Sienna began unwrapping the bandage on her left hand. Less than a minute later, she was on the verge of tears again.

…It's awful…

The wound was unspeakably horrible. Pink burns ran across the white back of her hand. The skin there was swollen and inflamed. She had heard that the burns had reached almost to her elbow at first. Although they had shrunk after the priest treated her, they remained severe.

A father did this to his own five-year-old daughter.

"I'm sorry—they're disgusting, aren't they? You shouldn't look too much," Brigitte said. Sienna's silence must have worried her.

"No…no, they're not, miss."

When the emerald eyes with a puzzled gaze met her own, Sienna felt ashamed of herself all over again.

"I'm sorry, miss."

"Why are you saying sorry, Sienna?"

"Because I did something terrible to you."

Brigitte must have still been delirious because she only blinked uncomprehendingly. Sniffling, Sienna wrapped Brigitte's left hand loosely in a damp cloth. By the time she finished, Brigitte's breathing had calmed slightly.

"Miss, is there anything you want me to do?"

"What?"

"If there's anything I can do, please tell me."

Until now, she had been defiant. Sienna expected Brigitte to be confused by her suddenly changed attitude, but for some reason, the girl frowned guiltily.

"I'm sorry," she said. "I couldn't see Father."

"I don't care about that… Please don't apologize anymore," Sienna said earnestly.

Brigitte reacted with surprise. "Well, um…there's something I want."

"Yes?"

"I feel so hot and heavy… Would you hold my hand until I fall asleep?"

Sienna stared wide-eyed as she timidly held out her right hand.

That's all she wants?

She realized that Brigitte didn't have a mother or a father to hold her hand at night when she had a fever anymore. She'd heard that the earl was already adopting another child. But Sienna didn't have a home to return to, either.

"Miss, this is your house now."

Sienna knew her words might sound cruel, and she thought maybe Brigitte would cry. But she just listened quietly.

"I— We are going to make this place a home for you."

So please, will you smile just a little?

She wanted Brigitte to be healthy and strong. She didn't want her to suffer. She wanted her to be happy. Those were her true feelings. Sienna squeezed Brigitte's right hand with both of her own. It was the soft hand of a young child.

"…Thank you."

"Miss?"

"Your hand is so cool…"

Brigitte's eyes slowly closed. Her breathing was peaceful. Sienna promised herself she would hold that warm little hand forever.

I can't believe that was eleven years ago.

By now, watching Brigitte grow up was the most meaningful thing in her life. The other cottage servants, too, felt deep affection toward her. Nathan the cook loved preparing her daily meals. Carson the pâtissier spoke roughly, but he made her smile. Hans the gardener had planted an ash tree that grew high to hide the cottage from the main house. Little fairies gathered in the tree, delighting Brigitte.

Still, no matter how hard they worked, Sienna knew the cottage was probably far from a haven for her. After all, she did not live there with her parents.

But even so, I…

"Miss, can I help you carry those packages?" someone suddenly asked her as she walked along.

"No, thank you," she replied curtly.

"Too bad," the young man said as she glanced over, although his smile told her he didn't really think it was too bad.

It was Clifford Yuize, Yuri Aurealis's mild-mannered attendant. She assumed his job was similar to hers—looking after his master's needs. He told her he was out shopping for Yuri.

"Would you like to join me for a cup of tea?" he asked.

"No, thank you. My mistress will be coming home soon."

"Ah, I see," he said, looking genuinely disappointed this time.

They had met for the first time a few days ago, introduced by their master and mistress, and it seemed he'd taken a liking to her. She couldn't tell, though, if he was romantically interested or simply thought Brigitte's blank-faced maid was amusing.

I suspect it's the latter...

"Then I'll walk you to your carriage."

"...Thank you."

It would probably be rude to turn him down again. She nodded modestly to the curious attendant. When she lifted her face, she found him unaffectedly taking her bags.

"Shall we go?" he asked. "By the way, have you heard? It seems Miss Brigitte will be visiting the House of Aurealis soon."

"...Yes, she told me."

"My master said he was going to set a date during summer vacation. Unusual for him to take such initiative!"

Walking beside her, Clifford smiled with amusement. But the truth was, Sienna felt incredibly worried about Brigitte. She had come to Sienna all red cheeks and bashfulness, saying, "Actually, you know Sir Yuri? Well, you see, he's asked me to his house," and now it was too late for Sienna to say she objected.

But if something were to happen to her...

Sienna knew that Yuri was a son of the illustrious House of Aurealis, and he would not likely harm an unmarried young lady. But she also knew that Prince Joseph, whose family held the highest position in the kingdom, had tormented Brigitte's heart for years.

"I will go with her, of course," she said.

"Yes, of course. I'm looking forward to that."

Sienna flashed her orange eyes at him, but he only smiled with genuine anticipation. She sighed. Perhaps it was none of her business.

"Mr. Clifford, may I ask you a question?" she asked.

"And what would that question be?"

She hesitated, then said, "...Do you mind having a name like Clifford?"

"Of course I mind," he answered without pause. But his expression remained calm. He touched his short light-blue hair. "But— what I hated was the House of Aurealis, not Sir Yuri. I understand now how meaningless it was for me to conflate the two."

His answer was brief, but the look in his eyes, as if she were shining gold, spoke eloquently to his feelings.

It seems we've both ended up working for good people.

Sienna bid Clifford good-bye and stepped into the carriage that took her home to the cottage. She changed swiftly into her uniform and walked straight to the entryway, then flung the front door open.

"Welcome home, Miss Brigitte."

Only someone who knew her very well would have detected the faint smile on her lips. Her beloved mistress, fiery hair glowing even in the twilight, smiled happily and answered, "It's good to be back."

Afterword

It's a great pleasure to meet you. My name is Harunadon. Thank you so much for reading *If the Villainess and Villain Met and Fell in Love*!

Since the full title of this book is so long, I call it *VillVill* for short. I got the idea for the book when I realized I might never have read a story where the hero and heroine are both Cinderellas.

When I look back at my scribbled notes, I see that I originally planned to tell the story from the perspective of a waiting maid and attendant whose respective mistress and master were said Cinderellas. At that stage, the main characters were named Sienna and Clifford, and they ultimately made their way into *VillVill*. I like the balance between aloof Sienna alongside Brigitte of the passionate Meidell family and sunny Clifford alongside the cool and composed Yuri.

Many spirits also feature in the book. At first, I thought of including only fairies, but strictly speaking, that would have limited my choices considerably, so I lost quite a bit of sleep over what term to use. Ultimately, I thought, why not jumble spirits and fairies together and call them all spirits in this universe? Why not make it one big party? After that, I was able to write without much hesitation. Although I have distinguished spirits from fairies in the book, I think you'll do fine if you just think of them all as spirits.

I've included spirits that are said to have truly existed in some far-off land, thoroughly fantastical spirits, and everything in between. I hope you enjoy reading about spirits who show up whenever and wherever they please.

As for the illustrations, I can hardly believe that Yomi Sarachi was kind enough to do them. I still cannot express in words how happy and moved I felt the first time I saw the cover illustration...

When I saw the appealing illustration of lovely, noble Brigitte and cool, sarcastic Yuri, I truly felt that I was meeting my characters in person. Thank you so much.

To my editor, F, I promise to keep working hard. I hope that you will, too. Keep up the good fight!

Finally, allow me to express my heartfelt gratitude to everyone who supported this book in its serial form on the *Shosetsuka ni Naro* website, and to you for choosing to read it.

I hope you'll stay tuned to see where love takes this awkward, impatient, irritable pair next. I look forward to seeing you in the next volume.